# WITCH BURGLAR IN WESTERHAM

*Paranormal Investigation Bureau Book 12*

## DIONNE LISTER

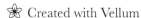 Created with Vellum

# CHAPTER 1

A wolf whistle trilled offensively through the room. I spun around and opened my mouth to give the culprit a dressing down. But then I stopped.

"Hello, gorgeous. Give us a kiss." The green parrot perched on a bird stand made kissy noises.

I laughed. "How did I not notice you before? You are gorgeous." I made kissy noises back.

The parrot bounced up and down. "Frank is gorgeous. Frank is gorgeous. Give us a kiss." Brief flashes of Mrs Soames's cockatoo, Ethel, threatened to ruin this interaction, so I pushed it out of my mind. Having that bird living with us was something I'd rather forget.

"As cute as you are, I'm not looking for a pet right now. Sorry, Frank." Frank cocked his head to the side and regarded me. Way to make me feel guilty.

Millicent turned from her conversation with the woman

at Feathered and Furry Friends Animal Shelter and smiled. "Why don't you adopt him?"

"Yes, because I'd love for Angelica to kick me out of home. Plus, I cherish my sleep-ins. If Ethel's anything to go by, I'd be up at the crack of dawn every morning. Yeah, nah. Why don't *you* adopt him?"

"He's not in love with me."

"Love at first sight doesn't exist, and he hardly knows me, so I doubt he loves me either." I pulled a silly face. "Besides, if I turned up at home with a new boyfriend, Will would be less than impressed."

Jane, the thirty-something-year-old running the shelter, laughed. "I'm sure you couldn't blame your partner. Frank is a handsome boy." She turned to the bird. "Aren't you, Frank?"

He bobbed up and down. "Give us a kiss." He wolf-whistled. Seemed I wasn't his only love. Was it wrong of me to be a bit disappointed that I wasn't as special as I'd thought?

Jane scratched his tummy, then turned back to us. "Okay, ladies. As I was telling Millicent, we had a whole lot of animals adopted out a couple of weeks ago. A lovely retired woman came in and scooped up ferrets, cats, dogs, a couple of birds, and rats. She has a farm and loves to look after rescues. While I'm overjoyed that they found their forever homes, it means we only have two rats for you to choose from, and we only have those because their thirteen-year-old owner's mother was sick of the smell. You really do need to change their wood shavings regularly. Follow me."

We wandered through the hallway and out a back door to a long room that looked like a converted shed. Cages on either side of the middle aisle sat on a concrete floor. Most of them were empty. I counted a couple of cats and three dogs. I stopped at the first occupied cage and bent to chat to an orange cat that was pushing its face to the bars, but Millicent dragged me onwards. Her face strained, she whispered, "Keep walking. I can't stop. If I do, I'll end up taking home a whole bunch of animals James won't want."

"Oh, okay." Understanding dawned, and her sadness seeped into me. She could hear the animals begging for love, for a safe, comfortable home with their own humans. I reluctantly let her sweep me onwards, like a piece of driftwood in a raging river. Maybe I should consider adopting an animal—it's not like our home was overrun with pets, and I'd wanted one for a while. Goodness knew I was home alone quite often, and companionship from a warm, soft cat or dog would be welcome.

Jane stopped. "Here we go." On top of an empty wire cage sat a smaller fish tank, which contained wood shavings, a nest of tissues, multi-coloured running wheel, and small water distributor stuck on the side of the glass. A caramel-coloured rat snuggled up to a dark-brown one that had a white heart-shaped spot on its back. "Here are Cinnamon and Bagel. Bagel has the heart on her back. They're gentle and friendly. They don't mind being handled and love to snuggle in pockets, but they might leave a present." She chuckled. I eyed the rats. I did not want poo in my pockets, no matter how small. "We do prefer they be adopted together. They're sisters, and in their six months of life have never been separated."

Millicent smiled. "Hey, girls." She bent so she was eye level with the animals. I didn't feel her magic, but talking to animals was her talent, so if she wasn't trying too hard, she wouldn't need extra power to do her thing. Both rats looked up, noses twitching. Mill looked up at Jane. "Can I put my hand in and have a pat?"

"Of course." She carefully took the glass lid off.

Millicent stuck her hand in. The rats tentatively approached it and sniffed. "That's it. Come on." She placed her palm up. "On you get." They looked up at her, and she nodded encouragement. They stepped on, and she lifted them out of the cage and up to her face. They touched noses with her. After a minute of her quietly regarding them and they her, she carefully placed them back in the cage. "I'll take them both." I wondered what their conversation consisted of. Had she mentioned she had a PIB assignment for them? Not that animals knew what the PIB was. Which led me to another question. Why didn't they have a special animal unit within the PIB? Talking to animals wasn't a common talent, but it wasn't unheard of. Surely they'd have two or three agents who could talk to animals? They'd be a real asset when fighting crime. The non-witch army, border security, and police already relied on dogs and ferrets.

Jane beamed. "That's wonderful. Let's fill in the paper-work. Have you got a cage and food for them?"

"Yes. I'm all sorted. Lots of fruit and veg and some liver. We're ready to add to our family." She chuckled. The liver part made me cringe, but I supposed someone had to eat it —better a rat than me.

After completing the paperwork and bringing a box in from the car, Millicent gathered her new family members. I slid into the passenger seat of her car, and she gave me the cardboard box to hold. "Are they okay in there?"

"Yep. I explained what was happening. They'll just sleep until we get home."

She shut my door, walked around the car, and got into the driver seat. She started the car, and as we pulled out into the street, I made a bubble of silence. "Did you grab them because they were the only ones, or do you think they can do what we need?"

"Luck is on our side. They're perfect. Most rats are smart, but these are super smart. They're suitable for familiars too, but I don't want them linked to me forever, so once their assignment is done, they can be family pets. Linking them as familiars would make things easier, and give them added understanding, but they're smart enough to do what I'll need them to."

"How long will they take to train?"

"A week or two. I'll find out what their favourite treats are, and we'll go from there." She chuckled. "In fact, if I had a few double-chocolate muffins, I bet I could teach you a whole lot of things." She smirked.

"Ha ha, very funny." I laughed in spite of the insult—it was made in good fun after all. And it was probably true. I made my voice high and mousey. "Squeak, squeak."

Millicent concentrated for a moment and glanced at the

box. She smiled. "Bagel said you did a terrible rat impression, and to stick to humanning."

I laughed. "Did Bagel say that, or was it you?"

We stopped for a red light, and she turned to me, her face earnest. "It was Bagel. Honestly. When we get home, I'll show you exactly how much they understand." She smiled. "It's like nothing you've ever seen before." Wow, if it was going to be more impressive than her talking a giant squirrel off a roof, this was going to be something. The light turned green, and I nodded at it.

As we took off towards home, I cradled the box in my lap. With a bit of luck, these cute little creatures were going to help us track down the leaders of Regula Pythonissam. After losing Graham, the politician, in an explosion in which his secretary and three others also died, we needed to ramp up our efforts. Their senseless murders were a reminder that we were dealing with a dangerous organisation that would stop at nothing to cover their tracks.

And we were going after them. With the help of rats.

I was pretty sure we could admit we'd fallen into a ravine of desperation. Were we going to climb out the other side, or would our enemies bury us there?

I closed my eyes and ignored the inner voice that whispered there was a good chance we'd fail. I could do without the negativity. With the wrong attitude, we'd disable ourselves and do RP's job for them. That wasn't who we were.

Not by a long shot.

# CHAPTER 2

After picking up the rats yesterday, Millicent wanted to give them a day to settle in, which we'd done. It was the next afternoon, and I sat on Millicent and James's living-room floor with a container of chopped carrot and apple while Millicent put the rats through their paces. Today was about figuring out how clever they already were, and how much time we still needed to put into their training.

Millicent kneeled on the floor, a small plate at her knee. Cinnamon sat in front of the plate, looking up at my sister-in-law. She spoke to it in English as her magic buzzed my scalp. Apparently, you could teach animals to understand English—or any language—if you helped things along with magic. Normally, she'd talk to them mind-to-mind, but we needed them to understand all of us. "Cinnamon, please take this piece of carrot and give it to Bagel, then return here for your piece of carrot."

Cinnamon's whiskers twitched. She grabbed the carrot off the plate with her mouth and ran across to Bagel, who was on the other side of the room. Cinnamon passed the carrot to Bagel, then hurried back to Millicent and squeaked.

"Good girl! Here you go." She held up the carrot —"Carrot"—then handed it to her. Cinnamon grabbed it and munched. Millicent looked up at me. "Any requests?"

"Hmm, ask her to run up to your shoulder, touch her nose to your cheek, give you a high-five, then stay on your shoulder until you say a certain word, then run down and wait at the plate." I would've requested something more ridiculous—okay, so the high-five was ridiculous, but I had limits as to how sensible I could be—but we wanted to train them to carry out tasks we'd need when infiltrating the factory in Manchester. After Graham's murder, we were pretty sure we'd find some answers in Piranha's father's business.

Millicent looked at Cinnamon. "Did you understand that?" The rat nodded. Nodded! Wow. "The word is 'go.' Okay?" Cinnamon nodded again. I really should be filming this. Cinnamon could be YouTube famous if she wanted to be. I'd have to ask her later. Millicent adjusted from her knees to sitting cross-legged and placed one hand on the ground, palm up. "Go."

Cinnamon climbed into her palm and ran up her arm to her shoulder. The cute little rodent touched her nose to

Millicent's cheek. Millicent held her hand up to the mouse, palm forward, and Cinnamon tapped her paw on it and sat back, waiting.

Millicent said, "Chocolate." Cinnamon stayed put. "Hamburger." The rat cocked her head to the side as if to say, come on, this is too easy. "Go." The rat bounded down Millicent's arm, leapt off, and stood next to the plate. "Well done, Cinnamon!" Millicent smiled and handed the rat a piece of carrot.

I clapped quietly, not wanting to startle the rodents. "That was awesome. Super impressive." Cinnamon looked up at me, and I could swear she smiled. A proud little smile that twitched her whiskers. I smiled back. What a weird world I lived in.

"Okay, your turn, Bagel." Bagel romped to my feet, looked up at me, then back at Millicent, who smiled. "Looks like she's chosen her partner in crime. Ready for a kiss and a high-five?" I didn't dislike rats, or mice, but having one run up my leg and arm? The jury was still out. Bagel squeaked, and Millicent chuckled. "Don't wait too long to say yes, or she'll get offended."

"I'm sorry, Bagel. You are terribly cute. I'm just adapting to the situation. I would… love for you to climb all over me." I smiled down at Bagel and rested my hand on my thigh, to make things easier for her. "Go." Her whiskers twitched in a flurry; then she climbed onto my sneaker and scurried up my jeans-clad leg. Surprisingly, it wasn't shudder-inducing at all. In hardly any time, she'd scaled my arm and was sitting on my shoulder, touching her cold, wet nose to my cheek. I held my hand up, and she high-fived me. "Pickle!" She stayed on her perch. "Go." She bounded down my arm and leg and hurried to Millicent for her treat. I smiled. "Pretty impressive, Bagel. Nice work."

She turned and gave me a tiny nod before munching her carrot stick. My eyes widened. I mean, I knew she understood, but such a human reaction? I looked at Millicent, who grinned. "I told you they were smart. I've enhanced their understanding with my talent. In connecting with them, I've taught them a lot about how we communicate— my magic flicks a switch inside their brains, in a way. It's complicated, so I won't go into the specifics, but once they've learnt this stuff, they'll always know it."

"But how can she understand me so well? I don't have that talent." Which was surprising since I had so many others, but I guessed I couldn't be good at everything. Damn.

Millicent absently stroked Cinnamon's back and cocked her head to the side. "Basically, in opening my mind to theirs, I've transferred my knowledge to them, at least for language. Each word comes with an image or feeling, so they understand it that way. And rats can understand concepts as well. At the risk of repeating myself, they're pretty smart to start with."

My brain was running to keep up. Maybe the rats were smarter than me now. I chuckled. "Okay, I'll take your word for it. Just don't ask me to play Trivial Pursuit with them." My longstanding dislike of the game was because I always lost, which I was sure I'd mentioned previously, but it didn't hurt to remind everyone.

"Promise I won't." A baby's cry came from the monitor sitting on the coffee table next to the couch I was on. My darling niece. Millicent jumped up. "Be back with my little princess in a moment."

"Don't rush. I've got all day, like, literally. Plus, I have company." I smiled at Cinnamon and Bagel. My friend circle was getting larger—okay, so they weren't human, but friends were friends. I wasn't sure if that made me desperate and pathetic or enlightened and lucky. Of course, I was going to go with the latter. I chewed the inside of my cheek. If I wanted to talk to them, how would I know what they were saying? I really was the inferior party in all this.

A knock sounded on the reception-room door as Millicent entered cradling Annabelle. I stood. "I'll get it." The security screen on the wall next to the door showed it was Millicent's cousin Daniel. I'd met him at the hospital just before Annabelle was born—he'd given Millicent a gorgeous rose-gold necklace with a heart pendant. Why didn't I have rich cousins? In fact, any cousins would be nice. I had a few in Italy, but I didn't really know them, having met them only once. Daniel knocked again.

"Are you going to answer that, Lily, or are you going to stand there daydreaming?" Millicent's tone was light, a tender laugh in her voice.

"Um, yep. Sorry." I unlocked the door and opened it. Daniel's sandy-coloured hair was still parted on the side but had grown enough that the straight fringe partially flopped over one eye. He jerked his head, flipping it out of his vision.

He smiled. "Hey, Lily. How are you?"

"I'm good, thanks. How have you been?" I stood aside so he could come in.

"Excellent, thank you. Work's busy, but I'm enjoying it, and Erin's well. Now, where's my gorgeous cousin?" I shut the door and nodded in the direction of the living room. He made his way in, and I followed.

Millicent grinned when she saw him. "Daniel! So lovely to see you." They hugged, and he gushed over Annabelle.

"Oh my goodness. She's grown so much! Mind if I have a hold?"

"Of course not. Just be careful." She handed her to him.

He cooed over her for a couple of minutes, then handed her back. "She's so cute. She's a good combination of you and James, I think."

Millicent smiled. "That's what everyone tells us, and we agree. So, to what do I owe this visit?"

"Well, Erin's thirtieth is coming up in three weeks, and I wanted to invite you and James to the party. I didn't want to call you about it because it's a surprise, and I didn't want Erin getting wind of it."

"I'm pretty sure we have nothing on. Having a baby has really put a dampener on our social life, not that we mind." She gazed lovingly down at Annabelle, who smiled and made a happy gurgling noise, which I didn't think would last long because she was due for a feed. That smiling cutie could easily turn into a screaming monster.

Daniel looked at the floor, then gazed around the room. My eyes widened. The rats! What would he think? Hmm, that was weird, they were gone, as was their paraphernalia. Maybe Millicent didn't want him asking questions. Or maybe she didn't want the baby around the rats, which was a fair call.

A trickle of magic touched my scalp. It was nervous magic with hints of something else I couldn't quite grasp— probably because it was such a small amount of it. A piece of paper appeared in Daniel's hand. "Here's the invite. It's got all the details." He gave it to her. "Oh, where's your necklace?"

Millicent put the paper in her pocket and felt at her neck. "Oh, I didn't put it on today. Annabelle grabs at it, and I'm afraid she'll break it. I do wear it sometimes, but I've just been a bit careful. It's so pretty that I would hate for it to get broken."

"Don't worry. You can always magic it better." He smiled. "Have you put any pictures in it yet?"

She smiled. "Yep. I bet you can guess the subject." He grinned at Annabelle. "Yep, that's right."

"Well, just make sure you wear it. Erin's funny about that stuff. She'd be disappointed if she knew you were so worried about it that you couldn't wear it. I'll tell her you had it on. Little white lie, and all that." He folded his arms. "Anyway, I guess I'd better get back to work. We've been extremely busy lately. I guess it's why I get paid the big bucks." He turned to me. "See you next time, Lily."

"See ya."

Millicent gave him a quick hug and reassured him she'd wear her necklace. Then Daniel stepped back, made his doorway, and walked through. Millicent looked at me. "I guess it's feeding time. Then I'm going to have a bit of a play with her. Mind if we get back to training tomorrow? I'll do some work with them tonight, after this one's in bed."

I shrugged. "It's your call. You're the animal whisperer, squirrel herder." I laughed. "I'll go home and get stuck into a Pilates video. What time tomorrow?"

"I'll text you later. Not sure if I'll have any other work on. I know Angelica's trying to keep me available to deal with this, but if something urgent comes in…."

"Yep, I get it. Not a prob. I'll see you soon." I gave Millicent a quick hug, and Annabelle grabbed my ponytail. I stroked her smooth, chubby cheek, then placed a kiss on it before reclaiming my hair. "You've got a strong grip, little terror." She gave me a gummy smile, and I melted into a puddle. "How do you guys ever say no to her?"

Millicent laughed. "It's not always easy, but we manage." She winked. "See you tomorrow, hopefully."

"See you both then. Oh, and if you need a babysitter for your cousin's party, I'm first in line."

"Thanks, sweetness. I really appreciate it. I'll let you know once I've run the date by James, but you'd be our first choice anyway. My parents come in second."

My smile was sad—yay that I was first, but boohoo that my parents weren't even in the equation. I sighed. Was this ever going to get easier? "Okay. See you later." I made my doorway and went home.

# CHAPTER 3

Back at Angelica's, I'd done my Pilates and showered, and I'd set the fire up in the living room. I lounged in my comfy armchair whilst reading a romantic comedy. There was a good thriller on my iPad, but that was too much like my real life, and I wasn't in the mood. The two characters were about to enjoy their first kiss, and I was engrossed.

Something landed on my head. I jumped up, screamed, turned, and swung my iPad. Will jumped back, his mouth and eyes wide open. "It's only me, Lily. Put the device down."

I stopped waving my iPad and breathed heavily. "Damn you, Agent Crankypants. Don't blooming sneak up on me like that. Are you trying to kill me?"

He chuckled. "Are all Aussies such drama queens."

I put my iPad on the chair and slammed my hands onto

my hips. "Are all Englishmen such inconsiderate crapheads?"

He laughed. "Touché."

"What are you doing home in the middle of the afternoon anyway?" My voice still held a spark of annoyance. I wouldn't calm down until my heart rate stabilised.

He held his hands up. "I come in peace. Honestly." He grinned and showed his dimple.

I narrowed my eyes. He so wasn't playing fair. "Okay, so spill."

"I have a local case to check out, and I'm going to have to drive. Thought you might want to come with me, and we can grab something from Costa afterwards. Are you in?"

I smiled. "Of course I'm in. You said the magic word."

"Costa?"

"Yep." I magicked my houndstooth jacket on. March was still pretty cold in Westerham. Back home, in Australia, it was oscillating between summer and autumn—some days would be in the thirties and some in the low twenties, but here it was mostly below twelve, which was pretty much the coldest Sydney day in winter, and don't get me started on the days it was five degrees. I shivered.

Will's brow wrinkled. "Are you coming down with something?"

"Huh? Oh, no. Just the thought of cold weather makes me shiver, apparently. Let's do this. Now that you mentioned Costa, my stomach is pining." On cue, it gurgled.

He rolled his eyes. "You and your stomach. Okay, come on, before your stomach eats you alive."

As we left the house, I donned my return to sender. Will, always the gentleman, even though I'd told him so many times he didn't have to, opened the passenger door for me. "Thanks, but you kn—" He placed his finger on my lips.

"Yes, I do know, but I want to. It's not always practical, like if it's pouring rain, but we have time, and I'm not unduly suffering for the gesture, so I want to." He gave me a quick kiss on the lips. How could I argue? I happily hopped up into the Range Rover.

When he said the job was local, he wasn't kidding. After no more than six minutes, we arrived at our destination—a dead-end laneway with ten houses on each side of the street. Two police officers stood on one side of the road, in front of a semi-detached bungalow. Six people had gathered in front of them, all talking at once. One short, sinewy elderly lady wearing a cream-coloured turtleneck and pink slacks waved her arm around, then pointed at a house directly across the road. One of the police—a young woman about my age with dark hair—held her hands up in a calm-down manner. The old lady lifted her other arm so that now they were both waving in a way that could be classed as vigorous exercise.

I turned to Will. "You'd better intervene before someone drops dead from skyrocketing blood pressure."

He chuckled. "You could be right. Let's go." I knew he wouldn't be laughing at her dropping dead—the scenario was much tamer than what he was usually confronted with. There was no immediate danger and no dead bodies. So far, this was a social outing as far as we were concerned. Ooh, and he'd given me the go-ahead to join him. I wasn't going to pass up the opportunity. When I joined him on the footpath, he said, "Just don't get involved. I'm letting you watch from the sidelines. Okay?"

I held my hand up, three middle fingers together and straight like little soldiers in a row. "Scout's honour."

He raised a brow. "That means nothing, considering you're not a scout."

I shrugged. "It's the best you're going to get. Besides, what could I possibly have to interfere about? It all looks pretty straight forward. I'll let you law-and-order types do your thing."

He gave me a deadpan look before heading to the group. I pushed my lips together to hide my smile—I wouldn't want the police or the irate residents thinking I was laughing at them.

I sat on a sturdy, low stone fence in front of a cottage a few metres from the scene. It was perfectly situated—I was a safe distance away, could see everything but not quite hear all of it. I made a spell that sucked the noise to me from that direction, ensuring I could hear them perfectly. I smiled to myself, proud at my tiny achievement. I'd never done that spell before, but I remembered it from going through the grimoire. Maybe I should make a list of all the spells I needed to try out—a conjuring bucket list. Hmm, that could be fun.

Will held up his hand as he reached the small crowd. No one quietened, and, in fact, the crowd surged around him in their efforts to earbash the police, pushing Will out of the way. His lips formed a line, and his eyes did that storm-cloud thing. I sighed—he was so sexy when he was angry. It bore remembering that he wasn't angry with me, so I could happily look on and swoon.

Will put a finger and thumb in between his pursed lips and blew. I slammed my hands over my ears and cringed. My spell worked way too well. That shriek of a whistle would've been loud even without the amplification.

Everyone turned to stare at him, the police included. Will crossed his arms. "Thank you. I'm Agent William Blakesley. I'm a government agent. We assist police when necessary, and it appears we've been called here this morning because you lot are too rowdy. Are you giving Britain's finest a hard time?" He stared them down, one by one. "Right. We'll have an orderly line, please. You'll all have your say… politely. The officers and I need to take notes and make sure we have the information we need." He looked at the policewoman. "I understand these complaints refer to thefts. Is that correct?"

She nodded. "Thanks for attending, Agent Blakesley. I'm Sergeant McKinnon, and this is Constable Forbes." She nodded towards a beefy, short male who looked to be in his twenties. "Yes, it appears a cat burglar's targeted this street. They've nicked an alarming number of items. We assured everyone that we'd get to them"—she narrowed her eyes at said "everyone"—"in their own homes shortly. But this lot are having none of it, I'm afraid. And that's making this more difficult than it has to be. We'll be here all day at this rate." I looked with my other sight. The young male officer was a non-witch, but Sergeant McKinnon was a witch. She must have contacted the PIB for backup.

"And when did all this start?" asked Will.

The old lady, who'd been one of the rowdiest, piped up in a shrill, crackly voice. "I called them a week ago. This is the third time they've visited. It's ridiculous. I'm sick of waiting for answers, and I'm sick of answering the same questions over and over. What are you going to do about this, Mr Hoity Toity Government Agent? Hmm?"

Will pressed his lips together, no doubt in an effort to contain an appropriately offensive response. When he finally opened his mouth, professionalism ensued. "I'm going to start by—" A mulcher started up across the narrow laneway, its grinding screams cutting Will off. The sixty-something-year-old man mindlessly operating the mulcher fed thick branches into the large contraption and paid no heed to the group across the street.

The old woman screamed at Will, her wrinkled face contorting as her mouth struggled to open wide enough to let the maximum volume of sound out. It was wasted effort —no one could hear what she was saying. Looked like she'd met her match in the mulcher.

It was time to turn my spell off, because I didn't fancy becoming deaf.

Sergeant McKinnon and Will exchanged a frustrated glance. The sergeant then turned to the constable and motioned for him to deal with Mulcher Guy. Will, the sergeant, or I could've concocted a spell to deal with the mulcher, but I supposed McKinnon wanted to fix it in an above-board way, and I promised I'd stay out of it. In the meantime, Old Lady was screaming into the abyss. One of the other men in the crowd looked to the sky, shook his head, turned, and left. Finally, someone with sense.

The constable was saying something to Mulcher Guy, but he couldn't hear, as evidenced by him holding his hand to his ear and pointing at the mulcher. Oh. My. God. Why were some people so oblivious? And by oblivious, I meant stupid. The constable shook his head, leaned over the machine, and turned it off.

Everyone was shocked into sweet, blessed silence by the sudden um… silence. Well, except for the old lady, who was screaming about her underpants. Say what? And why didn't she have an Off switch like the mulcher?

Everyone stared at the old woman, and it took all of approximately five seconds before they started in, yelling over the top of one another. Would a tranquiliser gun be overkill?

Will met my gaze, and I shook my head and frowned. He nodded, exasperation clear in his haunted eyes. I chuckled. This was why I'd be terrible at a public-service job—I had no patience. Wedding photography was bad enough when you had a difficult bride, but at least it was only once or twice a week, well, it had been before I'd moved here. Would I ever get back to being just a photographer?

The old woman, who'd been yelling at Will while he'd been looking at me, slapped his arm. My eyes widened. She'd just assaulted an officer, or an agent—same, same. I jumped to my feet—and, no, I wasn't going to strike her down with lightning, surprise, surprise—it was just a natural reaction. I was just ready to intervene if he needed. Okay, so he could defend himself against her no problem, but he might be worried about hurting her. I wasn't as worried. Wow, I sounded mean, even to myself. Would I change? Mmm, probably not.

Will's magic tickled my scalp. When he whistled this time, it was twice as loud as before. Yikes. Everyone shut their gobs. Finally. Even the old lady was standing still—her mouth was open but no sound was coming out. Yay! I nodded my approval, then sat back on the fence. Hmm, I was literally sitting on the fence, but it felt figurative too because I wasn't helping either side. Observing was hard work, or, rather, watching and refraining from helping was difficult. I itched to jump up and sort everything out for Will and the police. But it looked like Will had managed to get things under control.

"Right." He stared at the old woman. "Touch me again, and I'll arrest you. I don't take kindly to being assaulted." She pressed her lips together and narrowed her eyes. He looked around at everyone. "If you want to talk to the police about what was stolen, you'll do as you're told, or we'll get in our vehicles and leave. We may come back tomorrow; we may come back in a week or two. Who knows? It depends on our busy schedule. It's up to you." Ooh, I loved when he was all bossy, as long as it wasn't with me, of course.

The sergeant nodded. "Thank you, Agent Blakesley. Now, we'll come and see you in order of who is back inside their homes first." The residents jerked their heads around, glancing at their competition, before hastily scurrying back to their abodes. Even the screechy old lady toddled off with the kind of speed you'd only expect to see in the after-Christmas-sales rush. Sergeant McKinnon smirked, and who could blame her? She turned to her partner. "We'll deal with Mrs Horsham. Can you get started? I'll be there shortly." He nodded. The sergeant turned to Will. "Can you start with that house?" She pointed to one of the semi-detached bungalows on the other side of the street.

"Happy to. So, cat burglar, hey?"

She shrugged. "That's what they're saying. I called you in because not only is there little evidence, but we had a similar case about a mile from here last week. It's an ongoing investigation, but one by one, the whole street complained over a five-day period. It's looking like a similar thing here." She lowered her voice. "We found a magic signature in two of the ten affected homes last week, and I've noticed the same one in one of these houses. I have no idea what they used magic to do—whether it was to break in or move something large—but I've recorded it. I'll send you a copy this afternoon."

"Great, thanks. In the meantime. I'll deal with everyone on this side of the street. We can compare notes later."

"Thanks again." She shook his hand and made her way to Mrs Horsham's. I wanted to wish her luck, but she might not appreciate my humour. Not many people did. I could never work out why because, clearly, I was hilarious.

Will looked at me. I took it as a cue that I could attend the interviews, so I went over to him. "So, can I come?"

"Yep. You can be my note taker." He reached into his pocket, pulled out a pencil and small notepad, and handed them to me.

The door was already open, and the first victim was waiting for us on the threshold. The middle-aged man's hair was orange and arranged in a comb-over. I tilted my head to one side. How did he get it to stay? Was there special glue, or was hairspray enough to stick it down and stop it moving? Indeed, as the man—who introduced himself as Paul Goulding—shook Will's hand vigorously enough to make his own body vibrate, the hair didn't shift even a nanometre.

Will smiled. "As you know, I'm Agent Blakesley, and this is my assistant, Lily." Mr Goulding led us through to his kitchen, where a small table and two chairs sat. He offered us the seats.

I shook my head. "I'm fine. You two sit, and I'll stand to the side and take notes." I smiled at Mr Goulding. "Pretend I'm not here."

He shrugged. "Okay." He and Will made themselves comfortable, and I leaned against a wall, pencil poised. I'd sat on the fence for long enough, and I was a tad restless, plus I figured the interview would go more smoothly if Will could chat to Mr Goulding in a more intimate fashion. It probably made no difference, but you never knew.

"Mr Goulding, can you start by letting me know what was taken and when you first noticed things were missing?"

He tugged his earlobe. "Last night, I came home from the pub at half seven. I'd been there having a few pints with my mates from about, oh, three. My front door was open, and I know I left it locked."

"How can you be sure?"

He wrinkled his brow. "What simpleton goes out and leaves their front door open? I'm not daft. That door was locked when I left."

Will cleared his throat, but I hadn't missed the tiny smile before he'd smothered it with that seemingly innocuous move. "Okay. I'll check that out before we leave. Does the lock still work?"

"Yes."

"What else did you notice when you came home?"

"Well, as soon as I knew I'd been broken into, I went straight to my stash of valuables to check."

"Which was where?" Will asked. Mr Goulding paused and tugged his earlobe. With no answer forthcoming, Will probed further. "Well? You know I'm not going to come back and rob you later when you've refilled this secret hiding spot? And please tell me it wasn't under your mattress." Mr Goulding's brows rose. Will shook his head, and in a classic *Get Smart* moment, said, "I asked you not to tell me that." A chuckle welled behind my lips, but I pushed them together and managed to cough instead.

Mr Goulding's shoulders sagged, and he looked despondently at the kitchen doorway, then back at Will. "I suppose you want me to show you?"

"That would be helpful. Thanks. Before we do that, can you tell me what was stolen, and be specific with descriptions? Photos of the missing items would be good, if you have them."

"Well, you won't need a photo of the money. I had two thousand pounds in an envelope. Ah, and the two other things. I'm an only child, so I had my ma's and pa's wedding rings. The only things of value I had were under that bed." He hung his head for a moment before lifting it again. "After that, I needed a beer… the stress, you know?"

"I can imagine." Will's voice was understanding. He really was doing his best to be uncranky.

"Anyway, I noticed my favourite fridge magnet was gone."

I looked at his fridge. The only other magnet on it appeared to be one for a local plumber. Had his favourite one been from the electrician?

"And?" asked Will. Honestly, this guy was so bad at following instructions.

"And what?"

I couldn't help it; I rolled my eyes.

Will took a deep breath. "A description of the magnet, if you wouldn't mind?"

"Ah, yes. It was a koala, from my mate in Australia. He sent it a few years ago. He's since died… the big c."

"I'm so sorry."

He shrugged. "Well, what can you do? Anyway, that magnet was special to me. If there's any way of getting it back, I'd appreciate it. Surely whoever stole it won't try to sell it. I don't expect my parents' rings to still be there. He would've sold them for sure."

"We'll make sure to check all the second-hand and hock stores in the UK. We'll do whatever we can to return your items. Do you have a photo of the rings?"

"No. My pa's was a plain yellow-gold band, and my ma's was yellow-gold with a small solitaire diamond. They had them engraved on the inside—P & A 1955."

Will turned to me and gave me a heavy "look," his eyebrows lifting as his eyes almost bugged out of his head. "Lily, while Mr Goulding shows me where the things were taken from, I'd like you to wait here, and no selfies." What the hell? I scrunched my forehead. Then it hit me.

"Yes, of course." I glanced at the fridge, and he gave a small nod.

Mr Goulding laughed. "Young people these days. So vain. Selfies, selfies, selfies. I'd say I can't believe you'd sit in my kitchen and take selfies while your boss is doing an investigation, but I'd be lying." Ouch. That was harsh. Did I really look like I thought everyone wanted to see a picture of me in a stranger's kitchen?

I shrugged. Might as well play along. It was easier than getting offended. "Well, I have to pass the time somehow. And I wouldn't want my friends to get all the likes. We have competitions. The one with the least likes has to shout drinks on our Friday girls' night out."

He shook his head and stood. "Life was much simpler back in the day." What day? He only looked like he was in his fifties. He wasn't that old. Mr Goulding looked at Will. "Come on, then."

As soon as they were out of the room, I pulled my

phone from my pocket and pointed it at the fridge. "Show me the magnet." Sure enough, a little grey koala appeared on the fridge, clinging to a dark brown branch and gripping a gum leaf. The magnet was small—about the size of a matchbox. "Show me the person who stole the magnet." Nothing. I turned in a small circle, but there was no one. Had he merely misplaced the magnet? "Show me the person who stole his money." Hmph. Still nothing. Was my magic on the fritz? Nothing was out of the question. Maybe talents didn't last forever? I'd have to ask Will later. At least this wasn't a missing-person case or murder investigation. If we never caught the thief, it wouldn't be the end of the world. But still…. If that talent didn't work, would I lose my other magic? Now I was overreacting. Maybe there was another reason I had no result.

When Will returned, he gave me a nod. "Okay, Lily. We're done. Time to move to the next house."

"Bye, Mr Goulding," I said as I led the way out the front door. Will spent another moment reassuring him we'd do all we could to get his magnet back, and then we left. Funny how his friend's magnet meant more to him than his parents' wedding rings.

Out on the street, before we reached our next victim, Will stopped. "So, did you get anything?"

"No. Well, yes. I've got a photo of the koala, but I don't know if my magic is playing up. I asked about whoever stole the stuff, and I got nothing. I'm wondering if they didn't actually steal the koala and never went into the kitchen. It's either that or my talent is becoming unreliable. Can you lose a talent?"

He wrinkled his brow. "Not that I know of. Well, you could if you burnt yourself out. If you do that, you lose everything, but I've never heard of anyone losing part of their ability. It must be that whoever it was didn't go into the kitchen. Maybe his magnet is on the floor under the fridge."

Relief seeped through me. Thank goodness my magic was safe for now. "We should have asked. Oh well. Maybe we'll have more luck at the next property?"

"Fingers crossed." He headed two houses along and went through a small front gate set in a picket fence. So cute… the fence, not Will, although he was too. Credit where it was due.

A short, slim woman in her thirties answered the door, a taller man of similar age standing behind her. They introduced themselves and smiled. We were off to a good start. Will and I went through to Melanie and Tim White's lounge room and took a seat.

"Would you like a cup of tea?" Melanie asked.

Will displayed his friendly smile. "No thanks. We're good. We have a few interviews to get through, so we'd best get started." Melanie sat on the couch next to her husband. Will nodded at me. Oops, I'd forgotten to get the notebook out. Once I was set, he continued. "When did you notice things were missing?"

Melanie clasped her hands together on her lap. "Last night, just before showering. I went to put my wedding ring in the jewellery box on my bedside table, and when I opened the box, it was empty. I had two gold rings, a pair of pearl earrings, and two gold necklaces in there. All gone." Her eyes watered as if she was about to cry. "Those pieces all had sentimental value. One of the rings was my grandmother's, and the other was the first jewellery Tim had ever bought me. One of the necklaces was a gift from my aunt, and the earrings were my grandmother's from my dad's side of the family." Her husband rubbed her back.

"Do you have photos of any of the pieces?" Will asked.

Melanie started to answer. Shooting pain lanced my wrist, and I dropped the pad and pencil and gripped the stupid tattoo with my other hand. I had no idea what Melanie was saying because all I knew was the pain. Bloody RP. I doubled over my arm and rocked back and forth.

"Lily... Lily, are you okay?" Will was in my face. He glanced down at my arm, and his eyes widened. A stronger spike of pain gripped my arm, and it was as if my bones were on fire. I moaned and shut my eyes tight. I was sure I was putting on a spectacular show and scaring the hell out of the Whites, but there was nothing I could do about it. The pounding of footsteps vaguely registered. Maybe Will had run outside to see if someone was there.

I barely noticed the tingle of his magic on my scalp as I panted through the excruciation.

The pain stopped.

Oh my God. I breathed huge gulps of air but stayed curled over my lap. Waiting. I chanted at the pain, *Please don't return. Please don't return.*

Melanie asked from in front of me, "Are you all right, Lily?"

I gingerly unfurled and looked up at her. I wiped the tears from my cheeks. "I'm okay. I have a stomach condition that gives me really, really bad pain sometimes. I never know when it's going to hit."

She nodded. "Do you need anything?"

Will walked back in. "Ah, no. It's okay. Will just ran out to get my medicine. Can I have a glass of water, please?"

"Of course you can." Melanie hurried out while her husband looked at me, sympathy in his gaze.

I looked at Will, hoping my eyes conveyed the question of whether he'd seen anyone. "You did get my pills, right?"

He tipped his chin, which was a non-answer if ever I'd seen one. Either he'd seen nothing, or something had happened, and he couldn't explain. His magic tingled my scalp again. "Here you are." He pulled a small, white bottle of pills out of his pocket and undid the cap. He handed me a small pill.

I took it. "Thanks."

Melanie returned with the glass and handed it to me. I put the pill on my tongue and swallowed it with a sip of water. What had he gotten me? Since we couldn't just steal stuff, it must have been something from home. It could have been anything from fibre to a headache tablet. He put the bottle back in his pocket. "Are you okay now?"

I nodded. "Yes. Sorry about that."

"Don't apologise." He sat back next to me and looked over at Melanie and her husband. "Let's get on with this, then." It was difficult to focus—what if whoever had been out there was waiting to strike again—but this information had to be recorded if we wanted to get to the bottom of the burglaries. "So, you were both home when the jewellery was taken?"

Tim answered. "We assume so. We'd been out in the morning for about an hour, but that was it. Nothing looked untoward when we returned."

"Does anyone else have a key to your house? A cleaner or relative?"

Melanie chuckled. "If only we had a cleaner. Unfortunately, no. Well, Tim's mother has a key for emergencies, but she lives an hour away, and apart from there being no way she'd steal from us, she'd never come all this way and not see us."

Tim nodded, a fond smile on his face. "She also tends to stay the night when she visits. She's in her seventies, and driving all that way tires her."

"Can you show us your room?"

"Sure." Tim rose as did Melanie, and we followed them into their bedroom. Tim stopped in front of a dresser that sat under two windows.

"Were the windows open yesterday or last night?" Will asked. I shivered just thinking about it. Winter had barely begun to shuffle off—early spring nights, and days come to think of it, were still absolutely freezing.

Melanie shook her head. "Definitely not. I haven't opened those windows for four months."

Will did a quick once-over of the windows. "Okay." Will

turned to me. "Can you photograph the area—the access and container."

"Sure thing." I slid my phone out of my pocket. Even though it wouldn't matter, I had to at least pretend I was photographing the scene like a normal person. "Does everyone mind getting out of the way? I'll need to get a shot of the whole room as well as that area."

Will moved to stand next to me near the door. He looked at Tim. "Forensics will turn up later and dust for prints. After we get these photos, we're done."

"Okay, thanks." Tim took his wife's hand, and they waited just outside the door, in the hallway.

I silently implored my magic, *Show me the person who took the jewellery*. A sense of déjà vu took hold, but I shook it off. It was only last month that we were popping from country to country in search of Will's sister's friend and the stolen diamond jewellery. Which reminded me, Sarah and Lavender were coming to dinner the night after next. I still hadn't decided what to cook. Eggplant lasagne would be yummy.

Will cleared his throat. I blinked. *Oops.* His smile wasn't unkind, and I shrugged, giving him a grin. Okay, back to work. I focussed on the phone screen. I frowned and scrunched my forehead. Nothing. What the hell was going on? Had my talent deserted me? If only it had "desserted" me. I could go a double-chocolate muffin, pavlova, or lemon meringue pie about now, or maybe a bit of all three. Failing-at-magic-induced-stress eating. We needed a single word that encompassed stress eating. *Streating*. That covered it, although it almost sounded like streaking, and I was not going to do that. Nope.

I bit my top lip, then looked up at Will, everything I needed to say emanating from my eyes. "Okay, I'm done. I might take a shot from outside too. It will help us build a profile of what kinds of houses the burglar is hitting."

His brow wrinkled. "Okay. I'm done inside too." I would've offered to go out by myself, but with someone from RP lurking, there was no way I was going without a protector. We said goodbye to Tim and Melanie, Will assuring them we'd get back to them as soon as we knew anything and confirming the forensics team would be by later.

Stomach clenched into a ready-to-explode ball of unease, I gazed up and down the laneway, making sure I wasn't about to cop a burning arm. Confident we were the only ones out here, I crossed the road, Will next to me. Once on the other side, I turned, faced the house, and held my phone up. "Show me who took the jewellery." The screen turned dark, and I sucked in a breath. My talent hadn't given me the cold shoulder! The nearest street lamp was four houses away, and not much of it illuminated the front of the home. The light was on in the bedroom we'd just been in. A warm yellow glow shone from the small gap between the blinds and window frames.

Barely visible in front of the window was a stooped figure. Finally, something.

Maybe I hadn't been shown anything inside because the thief had magicked the stuff to themselves out here? I clicked off a shot and moved closer, clicking off another one. The person was about my height and all in black, including a balaclava. They might have been taller than me except for rounded shoulders and bad posture. I took one more shot from close up, and then I was done.

As we walked to the next house, I gave Will the phone and made a bubble of silence. "I wasn't getting anything inside. I worried I'd lost my talent."

He flicked through the images and handed the phone back. "I told you; it doesn't work like that. There's obviously a reason, and that's probably that the thief managed to do everything from outside."

"Yeah, I figured once that last scene showed up."

At the front fence of the next home, a sharp, old-lady voice stopped us dead. "Wait up." Will and I shared a look that said, Oh, crap, it's Mrs Horsham. We turned. She'd almost reached us from across the road. "When are you coming to my house, then?" When she caught up to us, she put her spidery hands on her hips. Actually, her hands reminded me more of that alien thing that grips onto people's faces. They were like pale lobsters. I really hated my memory sometimes.

Instead of trying to placate her with a smile, Will put on his crankypants face. Ah, that was the Will I knew from before I actually knew him. Yep, that made total sense. "I thought the sergeant had already interviewed you?"

She pursed her lips for a moment, then pointed a prickly finger at Will. "Never you mind what you think. I insist on a thorough job. I don't trust those police. Years ago, I went to them when someone stole my garden gnomes. They never looked into it. Useless, I tell you. Their badges aren't worth the paper they're printed on." Um, badges weren't printed on paper, and I was pretty sure British police didn't wear them anyway. Dealing with crazy was all in a day's work for law enforcement. Exhibit A stood before us, stance wide, suggesting she'd plant herself there until we agreed to her demands.

"If people are interviewed twice, we're wasting valuable resources, and someone else might miss out."

"Well, let them miss out. I paid my share of taxes over the years, young whippersnapper. I deserve it more than the younger generation. All they care about is selfies and plumped-up lips."

A muscle in Will's jaw ticked. I resisted the urge to rub circles on his back. Mrs Horsham would definitely find something wrong with that, and I didn't want to erode any kind of authority he had here, even if she'd already disrespected him. "What was taken from your home?" Gah, he caved.

"Mervin, my cat."

I couldn't help myself. "Are you sure he didn't just run away?" *Because you're mean and your voice is scary.*

"He loves me, and why wouldn't he? I've had him for five years. Found him in someone's front yard one day. I saved him from a life on the streets."

"In someone's front yard? Are you sure he's not their cat? Did you steal someone's cat?"

"Lily." Will's low tone held a warning.

"What? What if she stole someone's cat?"

"I did not steal someone's cat! He's my cat. I love him. I feed him, brush him, give him baths." Wow, baths. Cats could bath themselves last time I checked. Unless he was one of those Asian fishing cats, he probably didn't appreciate being dunked. She glared at me, then turned her attention back to Will. "Well? Are you going to help me get my Mervin back? He's black and white. Here's a picture." She pulled a picture out of her trouser pocket and held it up to Will. Merv was a fat black-and-white cat whose facial expression could be described as over it. He had a blue cardigan on and a blue bow around his neck. If there was one thing cats hated more than baths, it was wearing clothes. I'd never owned a cat, but one of my friends from school had. She tried to put it in a doll's dress once. The scratches had taken three weeks to heal. She never tried to dress Pringle again.

"I'll add him to my list." Will gave her a strained smile. "Now, we need to—"

She shoved a piece of paper in front of his face. "This is my phone number. Call me tomorrow; let me know how you're getting on. I don't know how much longer I can live without my little boy." She sniffed once, as if she was trying her best to care. But she must care, or she wouldn't be out here pleading. Unless she was just one of those people who liked to be difficult. Maybe she was lonely and wanted interaction? Who could say?

"I'll be sure to call you when we know something, Mrs Horsham. Good afternoon." Will looked at me, turned, and made his way to our next appointment. I gave Mrs

Horsham a quick wave and followed Will. I wasn't sure if I felt sorry for her or not. I kind of did, but I also found it hard to believe someone so bossy and cranky had a tender heart. When I imagined her heart, it was spikey and emanated tinny echoes when tapped. Okay, so I was quick to judge. Maybe she'd suffered a lot in life, and that's why she was how she was. I sighed, slipping into feeling sorry for her.

The next home was a small stone bungalow with a slate roof. Pretty little cottage. An old man answered the door, his hands twisted with arthritis, his legs bowlegged. He still greeted us with a broad smile and invited us in. "I'm Henry Wills. Pleased to meet you." He hadn't been part of the mob that had been outside. At least we were dealing with a civilised being.

Will went through all the usual questions. His missing items were a soft, fluffy bunny toy that one of his grandchildren had given him and a silver pocket watch. He had photos of both, which made things easier. Yet again, nothing showed up inside the house, but the magic signature was there, according to Will, and my photos showed that same black-clad figure skulking outside the home. One thing that seemed to match all cases was that the crimes, even though they'd occurred over two nights, had happened in the dark. Translocating things took a lot of effort, so it was probably easier if they were just outside, especially since they were stealing a lot of things. There was just one question I had for Will when we were back in the car after visiting ten houses, a bubble of silence firmly in place. Well,

I figured it was firmly, but we couldn't see it. I always imagined it to be like one of those clear bubbles people sat inside
and bounced down hills in. It would be cool if it was more
like a bubble that you blew, that was caught by the wind and
floated away. I sighed, then shook my head. I was really off
with the fairies today. "How did they magic the stuff out if
they didn't know where it was? I mean, if they'd never set
foot in any of the houses, how could they know? And why
couldn't I get a photo of them inside when four of the
houses had obviously been broken into?" Two houses had
open doors with no damage, but two had scratch marks on
the timber around the lock as if someone clumsy had tried
to break in, and magical damage. The whole thing was
weird.

"I can't answer that... yet. But that's what I love, the
challenge." He glanced my way at a set of red traffic
lights. "And we will get to the bottom of it. It's just a
matter of time." I was glad he was so confident, but I
wasn't so sure. At least the stakes this time were only small
possessions. We just had to hope it didn't escalate. The
light turned green, and Will accelerated. Without looking
at me, he said in a low, serious tone, "What happened,
Lily?" He didn't need to elaborate for me to get what he
meant.

I took a deep breath and blew it out. "The same thing
that happened the last two times. Intense pain. It was like
my bones were on fire." I held my hand up, my thumb and
forefinger an inch apart. "I'm this close to getting someone
to chop my arm off. We can attach a hook or something to

my elbow, and I'll be fine. It would make a good weapon, even."

He gave me an exasperated side-eyed glance. "Honestly, Lily. You're squirrel-brained sometimes. That's a terrible idea."

"I'm taking that as a compliment, by the way. In my next life, I'm coming back as a squirrel, unless I manage to turn myself into one in this life. I can roam and dart with my cute nervous brothers and sisters." I gave him a serene smile.

"You're looking a little too relaxed for the squirrel life. You'll need to up the manic a little. Get the outside as messy as the inside, and you'll be right."

My mouth dropped open. I narrowed my eyes. "You'll pay for that. When you least expect it, expect it." I gave him a mysterious look and waggled my eyebrows. He laughed. Grr, that was not the reaction I was going for.

"I still love your squirrel brain. Don't worry. Oh, look. Costa!" I looked out my window, and sure enough, there it was. I smiled. Will chuckled. *Hang on a minute.* I turned my head slowly to look at him as he found a car space. He parked and cut the engine. "You are so easily distracted, squirrel girl."

"Just don't be surprised when I steal your nuts and bury them for the winter." I drew on a small bit of magic and willed his underpants to heat up a little to emphasise my point. His eyes widened.

"Hey, get out of my pants!"

I stopped the spell and burst out laughing. "Just letting

you know this little squirrel has tricks. Be nice." I stuck my tongue out.

He grinned and shook his head. His happiness faded away, and he returned to Mr Serious. "In all seriousness, Lily, what are we going to do about RP? Do you think they're doing any permanent damage to your arm?"

I shrugged, lifted it, and prodded it with my other hand. "Nothing hurts, so I don't think so, but it is inconvenient to basically drop whatever I'm doing to writhe in pain. It's getting old. Did you see anyone when you ran outside when it happened?"

"I saw a car drive away, a white van. It didn't have a number plate."

Gah, not again. "So it's one of their henchmen. Aren't they sick of us killing them? I wonder how often they have to recruit." At this point, bravado was a legitimate coping strategy.

Will smiled. "Atta girl. Stay positive. If I catch them, they'll regret every bad thing they've ever done." His grey eyes burned with intent. "I won't stop until we've neutralised them all, Lily. I promise." He cupped my cheek and rubbed his thumb along my bottom lip. "If anything permanent happened to you...." He shook his head, determination in his gaze. "Come on. We won't stay long, but you deserve your treats." Hmm, neutralise could be anything from catching them and locking them in jail to killing them. Whatever we managed, I'd take it.

I smiled to let him know I wasn't nearly ready to give up. As I got out of the car, I looked every which way, making sure no one suspicious was anywhere near. And if they were, they'd better watch out. Will, despite uttering the word "neutralised," would probably prefer to catch them and lock them in jail, but I wasn't so nice. As much as I hated killing people, I knew my tally would go up, and to be honest, I wouldn't be sorry about all of them. They stole my parents from my brother and me. They'd made my life as difficult as they could. I was normally a patient person, someone who gave everyone a second chance, and sometimes even a third, but once someone crossed that line, went too far, I was done.

And when that happened, all bets were off.

# CHAPTER 4

The next day, we were all settled around the PIB conference-room table. I sat in between Will and Imani, while Liv sat in between James and Beren. Millicent was at the foot of the table, and our idiot in chief, Chad Williamson the Third, was in his throne—he'd upgraded the previous chair to a black leather one with gold-tasselled trim around the back support and red-fox fur on the arms—at the head of the table. Ma'am sat poker-faced in the seat to his left. He was gross. That poor fox. Sadness and anger narrowed my eyes. What a jerk.

Chad called the meeting to order. He leaned back, rested his hands behind his head, and clomped his heels on the table, knocking over his full glass of water, which flowed across the table. I rolled my eyes. There was no point hiding my disgust if he wasn't going to hide his disrespect of proto-col... and foxes. He was so incompetent that he probably wouldn't pick up on my cues anyway. Without sitting up straight, he waved his arm, and his magic prickled my scalp. The glass and water disappeared.

"Right, team, what have you got for me today?" So, he hadn't read the meeting sheet. Why was I surprised?

Ma'am sat up straighter, if that was even possible. Maybe she was sitting doubly stiffly to make up for Chad's sloppiness? "We're investigating, on request from Kent Police, a case of cat burglary." That was a funny term. I wondered where it originated. I mean, a cat had supposedly been stolen, but, of course, she wasn't referring to Mrs Horsham's black and white moggy. "So far, we've had reports of stolen items in three different streets within a three-mile radius of Westerham. The same magic signature was found at a number of these homes, but not all. Items stolen include jewellery, fridge magnets, plush toys, cash, wallets, purses, and a couple of pets."

"You mean more than one animal went missing?" I interrupted, forgetting protocol. I shot my hand in the air as Ma'am scowled.

"Normally, the hand goes in the air before the interruption, Lily."

"Sorry. I got carried away." Her look asked, what else was new?

"According to information, a cat and a ferret were both stolen. Although we can't say whether or not they just escaped, but since they're on the list, I'm mentioning them." Her magic tingled my scalp, and paper appeared in front of everyone. "Those are photos of any items we could get our hands on, as well as a list of all the items along with detailed descriptions. Study it well. Then I'm going to have agents Jawara and Bianchi"—she shot a look Millicent's way—"to chase up all the pawnshops around here, fanning out to include the whole of the UK." Ma'am looked at Will and me. "I'd like any more interviews to be conducted by Agents Blakesley and DuPree, and you can take Lily with you for note-taking support." Chad had no idea that the guys could record interviews with their phones if they wanted to. Note taking was as good a cover as any for me being there to take photos.

Chad's feet flew off the table and hit the floor. He slapped the table with a palm, making half of us jump. Ma'am, however, remained calm, a raised eyebrow her only reaction. "You have it sorted, then. I'll leave you to it. Oh, and Angelica, don't forget our meeting at two."

She blinked. Hmm, that might be a sign of surprise or distaste, or it could just be that she needed to blink. One could never tell with her. "Of course, Sir."

He stood. "Right. I'll see you all later. Happy hunting." He walked out the door. Happy hunting, indeed. He was so irritating. That fox fur on his chair. Argh. One corner of my lip lifted in a sneer.

Liv laughed. "Show us what you really think."

"You know I can't help it."

"And that's one reason you'd make a terrible agent." My brother winked from across the table.

"Who are you trying to kid?" asked Liv. "That's the only reason she'd make a terrible agent… oh, and her impatience and disregard for authority. Um… okay. Explain to me again, Ma'am, why you keep asking her to join?"

I sighed. Good friends were hard to find.

Ma'am smiled. "It's okay, Lily. You have great potential, but I respect your wishes." She made a bubble of silence with an extra layer of… something. Maybe strength? I had no idea because I'd never seen that little squiggly addition on the end, but the magic felt more powerful. "I won't repeat this, and neither should any of you because we don't want Lily being more of a target than she is, but I want to reiterate in case you need to hear this." Her smile faded, and her eyes were filled with earnestness and, dare I say it, passion for what she was saying. It was rare to see her display so much of herself, of how she felt. I wasn't sure if I should be happy or alarmed. "You're one of the most powerful witches I've ever come across, Lily. You could do so much good if you were an agent, but I fear you have other mountains to climb first. You are, at the very least, a valuable resource." Gee, thanks. She always knew how to turn something emotional into something dry and lacking as much positivity as possible. But she was giving me a compliment, so I should be happy. "You know I meant that in a nice way. Anyway, I just wanted you to know that you are capable, and despite your lack of respect for authority, you are a witch who could accomplish anything, and you have the grit to back it up. I believe in you. I always have, and I always will."

I pushed my shock at her praise out of the way and

basked in its warmth. Who knew when I'd ever get another compliment from her? "Um, thank you."

"Never forget my words. Promise." The intensity in her gaze prodded at the worry centre in my brain.

My eyebrows drew down. There was more to this, and if I asked, I'd probably get the brush off. Best to just promise and discuss it with everyone else later. I mirrored her intense gaze. "I promise."

She gave a firm nod. "Good." She pushed her chair back and stood. "Now, you all have jobs to do. Liv, if you can come with me, we have a few things to sort out with that gang case."

As Ma'am strode from the room, Liv stood, gave me a quick hug, and Beren a wave; then she was out the door too. My brother made another bubble of silence—Ma'am's having dissipated when she was done talking. "Meeting at ours tonight. Seven. Don't be late." He didn't need to say what it was about. We were back to having regular get-togethers about RP, and now we'd recruited our tiny spies, Bagel and Cinnamon, we needed to outline our plan of attack for Dana's dad's factory.

We all nodded. Millicent looked at Imani and said, "Looks like we've got some work to do. Best get started."

"Yep." Imani sighed and stood. "The only good thing about the tedious job we're about to undertake is that Chad didn't make Ma'am do it."

"Can't argue with that." Millicent nodded.

Will's phone rang. He pulled it out of his pocket and looked at the screen before answering. "Hello, Agent

Blakesley…. Hello, Sergeant." He stared at the far wall as he listened. "Of course. We have extra help today. Yep, we'll get on it straight away. Email the details. Cheers." He hung up and slid the phone back in his pocket. He looked at me. "If you need to go to the toilet and grab some food, best do it now; we have a huge afternoon in front of us."

Beren stood. "Sounds like that cat burglar's been busy. Are we sure we're only dealing with one? How many houses can one person hit in such a short space of time?"

"Twenty-five just last night, apparently. You make a good point, B. Lily only suspected one person, but maybe they work in a gang, and we got them after a 'quiet' night?"

I thought they needed reminding because they were so used to life as witches that they forgot witches had special skills. "But we're also dealing with a witch. We know whoever's doing this has used magic at many of the houses. It could be a speed spell for all we know."

Will shook his head. "It's most likely a translocation spell, considering we couldn't prove anyone had been in the houses."

"But what about the three open doors? They must've gone in. I'd say it's an invisibility spell, but you people keep telling me they don't exist."

Beren laughed. "You people? Lily, you're one of us. When are you going to start thinking of yourself that way? Miss Witch. It's about time, really."

"Beren's right, Lil. And stop thinking in terms of them and us. Other than secrecy about who we are, we're on the side of the non-witches too. The PIB is about justice for all."

Millicent came around the table and gave me a quick hug. "I'll see you tonight." She turned and left, Imani following and giving us a wave before she disappeared into the hallway.

I looked at Beren and Will. "Maybe I'm the bridge between the non-witch and witch world? I mean, I know I'm a witch, but I still feel like I'm an outsider at times." I shrugged. "Anyway, whatever. I'm going to have a toilet break and grab a sandwich and coffee from downstairs before we leave."

Will smiled. "Good idea. We can't have your grumbly stomach interrupting our interviews."

Beren laughed. "Yeah, you might scare the victims, and they've been through enough already."

I rolled my eyes. "Yeah, yeah, laugh it up." Damn, I had nothing funny to say. Geez, I hated it when that happened. They'd won this round, but I'd get them back later. I'd make sure of it.

# CHAPTER 5

I t seemed as if I went from one table to another.
Instead of a pub crawl, I was on a table crawl. After
what Will had fittingly called a long day of investigating, we all—with the exception of Ma'am—sat around my
brother's dining table ready for a meeting about RP. James
sat at the head of the table, being Ma'am's appointed leader
for all things Regula Pythonissam. I sat to his right, Millicent
to his left. Will sat next to me and Imani sat next to him.
Beren was at the foot of the table with Liv to his right, and
that was it. Warmth filled me. Everyone here was risking
their lives helping James and me find out what had
happened to our parents. They were also using their spare
time. Where would I be without these incredible peeps?

Oh, I forgot to mention our two new recruits who
currently hid in a shoebox on the table. There was a little

opening if they wanted to come out, but they were shy or napping in their nest of tissues.

James cleared his throat—he always did prefer the subtler ways of doing things. "We have a few things to cover, tonight. Firstly, we've obviously lost our line of enquiry via Graham Clarke MP. Things could've been much worse, though." He looked at Imani and me, still in one piece, thank the universe. That explosion still gave me nightmares. "Which brings me to Dana's father and his factory. Liv has been helping me dig deeper, and we have another lead." I held my breath. Was this the piece of information that led us straight to an answer?

Will grabbed my hand. "Lily, don't get your hopes up. Okay? This will just be another step in the right direction, and likely it's dangerous." My shoulders slumped.

James gave me a sympathetic look, his own angst emanating from his gaze. "Will's right, sis. This is another path to the next piece of the puzzle, but it's far from an answer to everything."

I sighed. "Okay. I knew this wasn't going to be easy when we started, but any good news catches me by surprise, and you know me…. I tend to get carried away at the best of times." My smile was sad. Will put his arm around me and squeezed. I breathed in the subtle aftershave mixed with the scent that was Will, and took comfort. There wasn't much else to do. "I'm good. If I haven't said it lately, thanks to all of you for helping James and me with this. You have no idea how much I appreciate it. And I realise what you're all risking."

Imani leaned over Will and grabbed my other hand. "Thanks, love. But you know we're more than happy to do it. You're important to the survival of witches everywhere. It's all tied together, RP and that. I'm sure it is. I don't talk about them, but…." She released my hand, looked into her lap, and pressed her lips together, maybe deciding something. Eventually, Imani looked up and into my eyes. "I have dreams. It's rare, but when they come, they demand attention. There's a battle coming in the witch world, and you're in the centre of it."

A violent shiver rumbled through me, and I swallowed. Her words carried weight. They sunk into me and turned my stomach to concrete. I wasn't superstitious, but what she said was real. I didn't know how I knew, but I knew. There was nothing I could say.

"I made a vow to protect you, Lily, and I stand by that. Even if I had a choice to pull out now, I wouldn't. You've become a good friend, and we'll get through this together. We all will." She looked around the table at the kind faces who nodded.

James ran a hand through his hair, then settled both hands on the table, palms down. "I'll second my sister's thanks. You're all acting so selflessly in helping us." He looked at Millicent. "Our whole family will owe you all a debt when this is over." I knew he meant that we weren't just finding out what happened to my parents, but it was personal for some reason—maybe that reason was that we were too powerful, or maybe they had a grudge against my parents? RP would stop at nothing to not only kill me but would kill my brother, his wife, and his child.

I blew out a big breath. Being reminded of the seriousness of our mission wasn't helpful to formulating a plan. "Okay, maybe we should move on from this kind of talk. I'll have nightmares and won't be able to think for weeks." I smiled. "And I'm pretty sure we'll need every bit of brainpower we can get to figure this out."

"You're not wrong there," said Beren. Ha, of all the times to be right, it had to be with the bad stuff. Beren turned to James. "So, tell us more about the new lead."

"I was going through our mother's diaries again, and there were three entries about trips to Mont St-Michel in France. One was a day trip they took, and the other was for a birthday dinner for Dana's father, the third had no explanation, just an entry that they'd gone."

"Oh, Mont St-Michel!" Liv's eyes lit up. "I love that place. I've only been once, but I'll never forget."

I looked at her. "What's so special about it?"

She smiled wistfully. "It's like an island. During low tide, it's connected to the rest of France by a thin strip that's above water, but when the tide comes in, the land is covered, and it becomes an island. It rises up out of the water, and from a distance, it looks like a fairy-tale castle. It's in northern France, so it's not that far."

"Nothing is that far when you can travel." Will winked. Ah, witch skills. We really could go anywhere we wanted. I'd really have to make time. Stuff RP and work. If I didn't start having a look around Europe while I could, I might miss out. Who knew when my time would be up? That sounded way more depressing than it felt. The fact was, motivation to do things was high at the moment. Even if I was slated as someone who could help witches everywhere, maybe when it came down to it, I'd have to sacrifice myself. *For God's sake, Lily! Stop with the morbid thoughts. You are not going to die, at least not today.* Ha ha, way to make me feel better, brain.

"In light of this, we need to organise when Lily can get to Mont St Michel. Depending on what you find or don't find, you may need a few days there to investigate. I'm just not sure on the timing. I'm leaning towards sending you there before we investigate the factory because if we're caught snooping around there, anything could happen, and since they figured out we were going to interview Graham Clarke and killed him, they might be expecting us. What does everyone else think?" His gaze landed on Will first.

"Um, I need time to think about it. If there is something about Mont St-Michel that leads us to them or an answer, they may still have ties to the area. Maybe they have surveillance? If they think we're onto them, you never know what they're prepared for. And if they're doing something illegal—which is almost a given—they might have surveillance because of that. Anything we do right now is risky."

I put my hand up. My brother wasn't anywhere near as cranky as Ma'am, but good habits and all that. "Yes, Lily?"

"Couldn't we pretend to have a holiday day? The other option is disguises."

Imani raised a brow. "That didn't work for us last time."

Hmm, she made a good point. We almost got blown to smithereens. "Then I got nothin'." Time to let someone else figure this out.

Millicent raised her hand. James gave her a nod. "I think we should send the rats into the factory. They won't be noticed, and maybe we can find some more clues that will help with everything else? If they don't find anything, we haven't given ourselves away, and we can plan a Mont St-Michel trip for Lily and whoever else should go."

"Sounds fair," said James.

Millicent smiled. "The other thing I wanted to do is introduce you to our two fearless rodents." She touched the shoebox sitting on the table in front of her and spoke quietly. "Hey, girls. Time to come out and meet everyone."

After a few seconds, a little nose and whiskers appeared at the box's small opening. Cinnamon emerged first. She stopped just outside the door and looked around the table before dashing to Millicent and hopping onto her hand. Aw, so cute. Bagel was next. She tested the air with her nose first, then came all the way out. She gazed around, and as soon as she saw me, her whiskers vibrated, and she squeaked. She hurried over to me.

"Aw, hello, cutie! You remember me from the other day?" I held my hand out, and she climbed into my palm.

Millicent laughed. "Looks like someone has a new friend."

"Lucky me." I smiled down at Bagel, who was peering at Will. "Do you want to check him out? He's a good friend. In fact, everyone here is nice—you can trust them all."

"Maybe not me." Liv had pushed her seat back and was as far from the table as she could get, which wasn't much since the wall was behind her. She tried to hide behind Beren.

I laughed. "Um, just stay away from Liv. She's nice but a scaredy-cat. And don't be offended—she's scared of big dogs as well. I guess she's just not an animal person, which, quite frankly, is disappointing." I smirked at Liv, and she narrowed her eyes.

The rat squeaked. Millicent shook her head. "No, she's not a cat disguised as a human. It's a saying. Don't worry, Bagel. You're completely safe."

I stroked her little head and down her back to calm her. Poor thing. "Don't worry about Liv. She really is harmless." Bagel nudged into my palm. Looked like she was really enjoying the pats.

Will gave Bagel a nod. "Pleased to meet you, Bagel. You have nothing to fear from me." She sniffed the air towards Will, then went back to snuggling in my palm. She must feel comfortable, which was nice.

James smiled. "Okay, now that the introductions are done, we'll formulate a plan for when Bagel and Cinnamon are in the factory. Millicent will need a couple more days for intensive training, and then we should be good to get them in."

Millicent jerked her head towards James. "Oh, and my father's developed tiny cameras for them to wear. They're crafted with magic, but once he finished, the magic faded, and they work like any normal transmitting device. There won't be any risk of us tripping a magical alarm."

"How do they wear them?" Beren asked. "If the harnesses are obvious, our ploy could be discovered."

"Dad's made thin harnesses the same colour as their fur. It blends in enough that no camera should pick it up."

Will leaned forward. "Speaking of your father, do you know when he can have another look at Lily's tattoo?"

Gah, why was he butting in? "It's okay, Mill. I've spoken to him, but we haven't set a date."

Will's brow wrinkled, his crankypants gaze finding me like a heat-seeking missile hell-bent on exploding. "Why not? You can't afford to let this drag on. I can't believe you're being so slack about this."

I looked down at the rat in my hand. "I think you'll need to hop onto my shoulder." Bagel climbed up my arm and perched on my shoulder, snuggling into the curve of my neck. I tamped down a smile at her antics because I was angry at someone…. Now that it was safe, I folded my arms and gave Will my determined stare. "I'm not being slack."

"Well, why haven't you done anything about it? I'm sick of seeing you in pain. For goodness' sake, Lily, we don't know everything that damn tattoo can do, and as it is, you're vulnerable to attacks. How many times has that tattoo incapacitated you in the past few weeks?" He folded his arms. Copycat.

"I know, but sometimes the cure is worse than the disease." I shook my head. "What Millicent's dad has to do is dangerous. He could die, or I could, or both of us. That's what I'm risking here. It's not as easy as you think."

He looked at the ceiling and pursed his lips before staring me down again. "I know that, but you have to do it sometime. Better now than later, and definitely before we find RP and confront them. How long do you think we have, Lily?"

I blinked, the truth slapping me in the face. This was really going to happen. It might take us another year, but it might only take us a few weeks to find RP, and hitting them as soon as possible was the best idea. The longer we left it, the longer they had to increase in strength or numbers or improve on whatever the hell they were doing to beat us.

Soon, I would find out what happened to my parents. But was I ready?

The scratch, scratch, scratch of fear in my throat gave me my answer.

No. The answer was no.

James looked at me. "I agree with Will. You can't even leave your house by foot or car without them catching up to you and doing something. They're obviously reminding you who's boss, trying to wear you down. Maybe they're testing your strength or trying to break you, make you feel helpless against their power?" He shook his head. "Whatever it is, we can't let it keep happening. If you were trying to fight them, and they did that, how are you supposed to defend yourself? We need this fixed."

Wow, James and Will ganging up on me—I didn't stand a chance. Unfortunately, I could see that they were right.

Man, I hated that. "Fine. I'll call him after this and tee something up." My stomach rebelled at the idea, and I swallowed the upheaval.

Bagel snuggled closer into my neck, her softness and warmth a welcome distraction. Millicent gave me a sympathetic look. "My dad is waiting for your call, Lily. He's ready to do whatever is needed. And you know he's good at what he does." Millicent glanced at James, then back at me. "If anything went wrong, no one would hold you accountable."

But I would. I wasn't going to argue the point. Millicent and her family were giving me a huge gift by being okay with this. I took a deep breath. "I appreciate that, Mill. I'm just sorry I can't fix it myself."

Will grabbed my hand and rubbed his thumb across my palm. Back and forth, back and forth. "It's not easy, I know, but you don't have a choice, and I have complete faith in Millicent's dad. The sooner you're tattoo free, the better. Nothing hurts me more than seeing the people I love in pain, and I've seen you in so much pain too often lately."

James nodded. "He's right. You've made the right choice, but make sure you follow through. Okay?"

I nodded. "Yes, fine. Okay. I'm going to call him straight after this. Now, let's move on."

Thankfully, we did move on, but after the meeting, James got Robert on the phone for me, and we teed things up for the next morning. I supposed that once the decision was made, it might as well happen as soon as possible. I'd better survive; otherwise, I was going to miss dinner with Sarah and Lavender, and that would really annoy me. I laughed at my idiot self. Well, a woman had to have something to look forward to in times of stress, or what was the point?

As Will and I travelled back to Angelica's, all the plans we'd made swirled in my head, but it was tomorrow that worried me the most. Because if I didn't survive it, the rest didn't matter, and if what Imani said was true, the whole witch world might suffer for it.

Well, I'd better survive, then.

# CHAPTER 6

I sat on James and Millicent's couch, my breath sawing in and out, in and out, two rats peering at me from behind the chair across the room. Sweat drenched Robert's flushed face, the alertness in his eyes a stark contrast to his slumped posture as he sat, his forearms resting on his thighs. Head held up with what appeared to be the last of his energy, he gazed up at me. "How do you feel?"

The last painful throb had dissipated a moment ago. I gingerly held my arm up, stomach muscles clenched in anticipation of the return of pain. But it didn't come back. I took the first proper breath of the last hour. A grin ploughed through my uncertainty. "Oh my God, it worked! More of the tattoo has disappeared!" I shoved my arm close to his face, making sure he didn't miss what I was talking about.

His grin matched mine. "That's fantastic. What a relief." Ha, that was the understatement of the year. "They shouldn't be able to attack you again, at least not with pain."

It was hard to believe, but he knew what he was talking about. I fell back into the couch, but there was no fist pump to be had because my limbs weighed a thousand kilos thanks to the exhaustion of our session. At one point, I'd had to contribute my own power to Robert's unravelling spells. It was as if I'd just completed an Iron Man Triathlon. My prize was one more piece of the tattoo—and RP's control over me—gone.

Millicent appeared at the door. "Did I hear chatting?" Her curious gaze flicked from her dad to me and back again. Robert smiled. "Oh my goodness! I knew you could do it!" She hurried over and gave her dad a hug and kiss on the cheek, then came and grabbed my hand, lifting it so she could peruse my arm. Her grin was even wider than ours. "There's only part of it left! That's incredible, amazing. Are you both all right?" She gently dropped my arm and stepped back to regard both of us. "I think tea, coffee, and some scones are in order."

Her magic danced down my nape, and a low table appeared in front of the couch. A plate of scones popped into existence, as well as small bowls of jam, and clotted cream, each with their own little spoon. A teapot, two cups and saucers, and a cappuccino also materialised. "Tada!" She waved her arm, and one of the dining chairs appeared behind her. She sat and poured a cup of tea and offered it to her dad.

I leaned forward and grabbed one of the small plates, and a scone. I cut it in half and spooned jam and cream on it. Mmm, this looked so good. I picked up my coffee and leaned back, ready to enjoy the spoils. Anything was heaven compared to the suffering I'd endured in the last hour. It'd been just as painful and exhausting as the first time, maybe even worse. I didn't know how I would survive a third time.

I took a sip. The warmth slid down my throat and settled in my belly. It was like a hug from the inside. I turned to Millicent's dad. "Robert, thank you. I know how much you're risking to do this, and I appreciate it more than you could ever know."

He smiled. "It's my pleasure. I live to serve, always have. I'm glad I'm playing my small part in helping you with your cause."

"You're playing a rather large part. Could you tell what the spell was exactly?"

He sipped his tea and watched Cinnamon and Bagel as they reached the foot of the table. I chuckled—they were probably after their share of the scones. Cheeky rodents. Millicent shook her head with a laugh and magicked another plate to herself and placed a few large crumbs on it, then lowered it to the floor.

Finally, Robert lifted his gaze to mine. "A mishmash of a few different spells, from what I could tell. Together, it was an attack spell that could circumvent return to sender." He shook his head slowly. "It shouldn't be possible, but they did it. It looks like it was possible because the tattoo had a receptor on it, so to speak. The attack spell was a feel-burn spell. The spell can't actually do any physical damage—it attacks the nerves so they send messages to your brain that you're burning. That could be the other reason it infiltrated the return to sender. Your magic couldn't see that it was going to do any damage because it wasn't actually written into the spell. It's complicated and a bit more technical than that, but you have the general gist."

Wow, there was so much I didn't know, and that made me more vulnerable. "Gee, what if RP have more of those spells? We could all be writhing on the floor in pain, and they could just come and handcuff us. Too easy." I frowned.

Robert chewed his mouthful of scone and swallowed. "No, I don't think that's possible. I think it helped because they had an anchor in the form of the tattoo. I doubt they could get past anyone's defences without that added bit of help."

"But can we be sure?" Millicent asked.

"No, we can't." At least he was honest. A light went on in his eyes, illumination that spoke of curiosity and excitement. "But we could test that theory."

I didn't want to be a guinea pig, but since everyone was risking so much for me, it was the least I could do, just not right now. "I'd be happy to be the testee. Maybe in a few days, when I've recovered from today?"

Robert smiled. "That's a good idea. Give us both a chance to rest. I know the threads of the spell, so I can duplicate it."

Millicent's eyes widened. "No! You can't go testing things on Lily. What if something happened?"

Robert regarded his daughter. "I'm not sure if you realise how strong Lily really is. I won't do anything that could seriously hurt her either, and I'd like to test this on more than one person anyway, but I think she needs to be one of them since you're sending her into battle at some point."

"Battle?" I figured clarification would be good. "I mean, I know we have to find out what happened to my parents, and that includes navigating some dangerous situations, but who said there's going to be any kind of battle? I thought we'd figure it out, and then Ma'am can get in there with her PIB agents and arrest them?"

Millicent and her dad shared a "look." I sighed. A "look" was going to kill me one day. Millicent turned her attention to me. She licked her lips. "That *might* happen, but chances are, they won't go down without a fight, and if they're as powerful as we think, we'll need all hands on deck. Which means you too. Haven't you been listening to Imani?"

Imani and her psychic abilities proclaiming me to be important? "Yes, I suppose. But that doesn't mean anything. Maybe I make the difference because I figure something out? Maybe it's my powerful brain she's talking about?" Millicent snickered. My cheeks heated. "I'm not exactly stupid, you know. Okay, so I'm not a genius, but I have a unique way of looking at things."

"You do, Lily, and you are smart. That's not why I laughed. You're just so cute when you're in denial. You are ever the optimist. I'm sorry if that sounds weird, but you really are underestimating things if you think RP are going to offer their wrists for our handcuffs. It's not going to happen. Your naivety is sweet, but it's got to go." She tilted her head to the side, and sympathy shone from her eyes.

I sighed. "Yeah, I'm an optimist. Let me live in denial a little while longer. Please?" She shook her head as if to say I was a lost cause. I looked at Robert. "I know you had your hands full unravelling that part of the tattoo, but do you have any idea what the remaining spell is?"

"I have to do some more research. It could be a number of different things, and I only have suspicions—I haven't settled on any one in particular. I'm not one for speaking unless I'm sure."

"Fair enough." There was a squeak next to my shoe. I looked down and smiled.

Millicent translated. "Bagel wants to know if it's okay if she comes up to your shoulder for a visit."

"Of course it is!" I reached down—which took most of my remaining energy—and she climbed onto my hand. As I settled back into the couch, she ran up to sit on my shoulder. "You know you're going to help us soon. I want to say thank you."

Her whiskers twitched, and she looked at Millicent, who then translated. "She said she's happy to. She says you're really nice… for a human."

I laughed. "Um, thanks, I guess."

Millicent and her dad had a chat while I ate my scones. I saved some crumbs for Bagel, who happily claimed them.

When we'd all finished, I magicked my plate clean and away because I knew where the cupboard was. Once that was done, fatigue hit me worse than before. Crap. I'd forgotten I was almost drained from the tattoo thing. When would I learn to think before I acted? And I still needed to get home. "Mill, do you think you could make my doorway? I just used my last ounce of magic. I need to go home and sleep." Bagel, who was back on the floor after I'd given her the food, looked up at me, whiskers twitching. She touched my shoe with a little paw.

"She said goodbye, and she hopes to see you soon."

I smiled down at her. "You're adorable, Bagel. I'm sure I'll see you very soon. And thanks for being so sweet." She scampered off. I had no idea where to, but it was probably to her shoebox to sleep. I slowly stood, dizziness engulfing me. I swayed but managed not to fall. I stayed still with my eyes closed until the spinning stopped. When I opened my eyes, a doorway had opened a couple of steps from me.

"Your chariot home, my lady." Millicent smiled.

"Thank you." We had a quick hug. I looked at Robert. "Thank you again. You're amazing."

He smiled. "My pleasure. I'll see you in a few days, and we'll run some tests."

"Sounds great." It kind of did, but it didn't. At least I could trust him, and maybe we'd learn something that would give us an edge over RP. There was a slim chance I'd suffer something, but hopefully, there'd be no accidents, and it would be fine. "Bye." I stepped through Millicent's doorway into Angelica's reception room. As painful and exhausting as today had been, we'd cut away another piece of RP's control over me. I smiled, renewed hope cascading through me in warm waves.

Maybe RP weren't invincible after all.

# CHAPTER 7

"Mmm, this is delish, Lily." Sarah pushed more of the eggplant lasagne onto the fork with her knife.

"You're one hell of a cook, but this is going to turn my waistline into a waistblob." Lavender patted his stomach.

I yawned. The nap I'd had when I came home turned into a six-hour sleep. At least my magic was recovered enough when I woke up that I could use it to cut the prep time short on the dinner. "Thanks, Lav. But what are you talking about? You're pretty much a stick. I bet you can eat whatever you like and never put on weight." Tonight's outfit was shiny, tight-fitting black jeans, and a tight-fitting lavender shirt. Silver hoop earrings, and a green-and-purple scarf finished off his look. Why couldn't I pull off things like that? If I wore what he was, I'd be mistaken for a clown.

He laughed and flapped his hand, batting away my

comment. "Sweetie, you are too kind. It takes effort to look this good." He gave a sultry wink, and I laughed.

Sarah put her fork down and sipped her wine. "I heard today went well."

Will grinned and grabbed my hand. He pushed my black jumper sleeve down, revealing my wrist. "Look. Only the head's left. She should be pain-free from now on."

I smiled. "Yep, except that the bit that's left, well, we don't really know what it can do. So I'm not snake-free yet."

"You'll get there." Sarah forked the last piece of lasagne into her mouth and put her utensils onto the plate into the universal arrangement for finished. She swallowed and sat back, putting her hands on her tummy. "Oh my God, that was sooooo good. I'll be full for a week."

"What a shame. Guess that means there'll be more lemon meringue for me." I smirked.

Lavender's mouth fell open. "How did you know that's my favourite? Ooh, you're so naughty, trying to fatten us up. Sarah could lose her job." He tried but failed to stop the corners of his mouth twitching up.

I shrugged. "She's a witch. She can magic the hunger away and eat nothing tomorrow."

She pouted. "Yeah, I'll have to, but you know it's not healthy. Gah, this industry is such a punish."

Lavender put his arm around her. "But you adore it, sweetie. You'd be sad without all the fabulous fashion and me. You'd miss it all."

She sighed dramatically. "Yes, but shhhh. Don't remind me until after we've had dessert."

I ate the last of my dinner and put my knife and fork down. "It's so good to see you two. We really should do this more often. Maybe Will and I can come visit you at some exotic location when you're working."

Lavender laughed. "You're welcome to come visit us this weekend. We're shooting a campaign in Birmingham."

Will choked on his drink. "Yeah, I'm just dying to go there."

"It's not that bad, is it?" I didn't know much. As far as I was concerned, everywhere in the UK was worth visiting—I couldn't get enough Englishness.

Will looked at me. "Name an industrial area in Sydney."

"Silverwater."

"Okay, picture it. Would you go there for fun, for dinner or lunch?"

"Um, no?"

"Exactly," Will, Sarah, and Lavender said at the same time. We all laughed. Poor Birmingham. There were probably some nice restaurants there, but I wasn't going to beat a dead horse and try and convince them.

"When are you in France next? Will and I are planning a little holiday in the north, but we haven't set firm dates yet."

Will's eyes widened. "Lily, it's only a maybe. We're not at the stage where we should be inviting people." He gave me his "shut-up" look. It made him appear as though he had a stomach ache.

Sarah tilted her head to the side and narrowed her eyes. "What's going on?"

Will sat back as if he were trying to move away from Sarah and the question. "Nothing."

Sarah's mouth dropped open, and she looked at Lavender, whose eyes had a knowing look. Lavender grinned. "Ooh, you sly fox."

I wrinkled my brow. Huh? Oh. It took me a while, but I finally understood. "No! He's not proposing. Sheesh. This was something I wanted to do." Yeah, I knew things should be kept secret, but Sarah was, well, Sarah, and my gut told me Lavender was someone we could count on to keep our secrets. I wasn't about to blurt the whole thing out. I'd discuss it with Will later. My whole point, which he didn't get because I couldn't explain yet, was that the more people who were there who weren't in the PIB, the more it would look like we were just visiting for no particular reason. Hmm, another thought was making itself known. What if we recruited Sarah and Lavender to our cause, got them to swear, but then kept them out of things and sent them on a secret mission by themselves. If they were careful, RP would never know what was happening. Although I still needed to go at some point to take the photos. But maybe we should show our hand with Sarah and Lavender right now?

I sighed. "Look I thought it might be a good idea, but we won't be going for ages. I keep forgetting how busy we are with everything."

Sarah's face fell. "Oh, poo. I was hoping you were getting married. You know it's going to happen one day. Why wait?"

My cheeks heated. I didn't know why, considering Will

knew I loved him. It wasn't like it was news, but… marriage? We were only young, and I sure didn't want children soon, if ever. Okay, so maybe I did want kids one day. If my niece was anything to go by, if I didn't have one, I'd probably regret it. But we were so far from that right now, what was the point in getting married? "I can give you a few reasons." Will frowned. Oops. "None of those reasons are that I don't love you. But we aren't about to have kids, and who knows? I could be dead in a few months."

Lavender's mouth fell open. "Lily, that's a bit extreme. I thought you only helped out with the PIB? It's not like you're an agent in dangerous territory all the time."

Will's eyes stormed into battleship-grey territory. His voice was low and fierce. "You won't be dying. Not on my watch. I don't want to hear you ever say that again." A shiver raced through me. It was nice to be loved that much, but could I promise? I supposed I had to promise, if only to make him feel okay. I nodded. That would have to be enough. Will turned to Sarah. "I wasn't going to ask her to marry me, by the way. Just so you know. I just hate making plans and getting people excited about a holiday then have to change everything because of"—he turned to me—"*work* commitments. You know my job is unpredictable, Lily."

Okay, so he was saying we didn't know when we'd be trotting off to France to investigate and that it was a bad idea to include his sister and Lavender. "It's okay. I *understand*." I gave him a look that said there was more to discuss later. I stood. "Now, who wants dessert?"

AFTER DESSERT, WE PLAYED PICTIONARY AND HAD A LOT OF laughs. At midnight, Lavender joked he didn't want us to see him as a pumpkin because orange wasn't his colour, and Sarah admitted she was tired, so they left. Now Will and I lay in bed, and it was time for the conversation I'd promised earlier.

I snuggled into Will's side as he lay on his back, and I rested my hand on his chest. I happy sighed. I mean, who wouldn't if they were cuddled up to a sexy, topless government agent with firm pecs. Hmm, that was something I never thought I'd think. I snorted.

"What's so funny? You're not laughing at my chest, are you?"

"Ooh, never. I like your chest… a lot. I'm laughing at myself."

"Ah, that makes sense."

"Hey!"

"You said it, not me." He chuckled, then made a bubble of silence. "So, missy, why did you mention our trip to France? You know it's not safe to take them. I can't believe you went there."

"I know it's dangerous, but I also thought that if they were there and thought it was just a holiday, it would make us look more normal and like we were actually there on holiday."

"Oh." I guessed an oh was better than an argument and meant I hadn't been totally stupid in thinking it might help.

"But don't worry. I've changed my mind." Would he hate my next suggestion even more?

"Well, spill. What's your new idea?"

"Who said I had a new idea?" I couldn't see him, but I heard his eyebrow raise. Yes, it sounded crazy, but I knew Will. "Did you just raise your brow at me?"

His voice was light. "Yes. Can't hide anything from you, can I?"

"Nope, so don't even try. So, my new idea. I was thinking we should recruit Sarah an—"

He sat up so quickly, my head fell into his lap. He reached over and turned on the bedside lamp. "No, no, no, no, and no. I'm not going to risk my sister in this. It's bad enough you're in harm's way most of the time."

As pleasant as it could possibly be with my head in his lap, I figured I'd better sit up. There were times for things, and now wasn't *that* time. I settled my back against the padded bedhead. "But she and Lavender could do a subtle look around. RP wouldn't even suspect them. It's not like they're even watching Sarah or Lavender."

"No. If anything happened to either one of them, I'd never forgive myself. Sorry, Lily, but we'll keep this whole thing agents only… and you."

"But what if we need more people as this thing drags on? We've already lost Ma'am, for goodness knows what reason. And we can't trust anyone else from the PIB. Maybe this is a job for people we can trust. Lavender and Sarah are both strong witches, and Lavender was so happy to help last time."

"Yes, but that was because two of his friends were in danger. We can't risk civilian lives." He turned to me. Even though I couldn't see him in the dark, I knew he was looking my way. "If my parents lost Sarah, it would kill them. They live with the fear of losing me, so it shouldn't affect them if something happened to me, but their little girl? It would destroy them."

I found his cheek with my palm... gently, not a slap. Seriously. I'm not a violent person at all, well, except when I have to kill people.... I rubbed my thumb back and forth over his chin, his stubble scratchy. "If anything happened to you, it would devastate your parents, and it would just about kill me. Yes, we live with that possibility, but it can't prepare you. Nothing can." I dropped my hand and sat back. He knew I knew first-hand. Not a day that went by that I didn't miss my parents, wish I could tell them something, or have a hug. Some days the ache was something I could push away, but some days it dragged me down into yearning so desperate that I couldn't breathe. Thankfully, the bad days were less than they used to be, and it helped having James so near.

He placed his hand on mine. "I still won't entertain that idea. They're not law enforcement, Lily. They're in the fashion world, which couldn't be further from a hardened crusader against evil."

I giggled. "You see yourself as a bit of a superhero, then?"

He growled, then shut me up with a full-on kiss. Seemed like I wasn't going to get my way with this. Hmm.... Did it even matter anymore? What had I wanted to say? Boy, his kisses were lethal for anything resembling coherent brain activity. My brain cells were all sighing on the floor. But I knew it was a good idea—call it gut feeling again. I'd just have to wait until tomorrow… when we were out of bed and my thought processes were actually processing.

If there was one thing about me, I was as stubborn as toddler who didn't want to go to bed. And sometimes, it even worked in my favour.

# CHAPTER 8

The next morning, we were up and dressed by nine. Ma'am had messaged that our interviews would start at ten. Another two streets were in uproar after having knickknacks, jewellery, wallets, and pets stolen. Looked like the gang of thieves were stepping things up. Surely they'd made a mistake and left some evidence behind in at least one of those houses. And why steal pets? Maybe they were pedigrees and they sold them later? Some of those poodle crosses were worth thousands. Who knew adding an "oodle" on the end of a name could be worth so much?

The first street we had to visit was in Sevenoaks. We didn't want RP finding out they couldn't hurt me through my tattoo—it might enrage them, and we wanted them to underestimate us. To prevent them from following me from home, Will was driving to a nearby landing spot, and I was going to travel there, where he would pick me up. I was still tired after yesterday's healing, but I had most of my power back, and travelling would be well within the realms of what I could comfortably do today.

About fifteen minutes after Will left, he called me from St John's Hill public toilets. They were only small, and even though we had a landing spot there, the toilet could've been occupied. Will helpfully went into the cubicle, made sure it was vacant, then called me. "All clear."

I laughed. "Thanks. See you in a sec." I made my doorway and stepped through. Pew! I coughed. Why did toilets have to smell so bad? I hurriedly opened the door to Will's smiling face.

"What took you so long?"

"Ha ha. Let's get out of here." I spun him around and pushed him through the door. I took a deep breath of fresh air outside. *Be gone from my lungs, germy vapour.* If you could smell it, you were breathing in minuscule particles of it. Yes, wee and poo particles had been partying in my nostrils. I shuddered. Gross. So, so gross. Sometimes I wished I didn't know what I knew.

We got into the Range Rover and drove another five minutes to the first street. Thankfully, there was no riot this time. Will's magic tickled my scalp, and a piece of paper appeared in his hand. "These are the addresses. Make sure you have your pen and paper ready, and I think we'll use your Nikon for this—it looks more official." I'd dressed in my PIB uniform of white shirt, black jacket, pants, and tie, but the more legit I looked, the better. My camera appeared, a comforting weight in my palm. As dangerous as it was going to be, I was looking forward to our trip to Mont St Michel. The pictures I'd seen on the net were amazing. I was definitely bringing my Nikon for that.

"We'll begin at the beginning." Will headed for number six, a two-storey 1950s brick home. A short, slim woman answered the door. She looked to be in her mid-thirties. Her longish blonde hair fell in styled loose curls, stopping at her cleavage, which was helpfully showcased in a tight-fitting, low-cut pink T-shirt, you know, just in case we might miss the fact that she had fake DD boobs. She smiled a tad too brightly at Will and didn't even bother to look my way. I didn't bother to hide my sigh.

Her voice was sweeter than condensed milk. Damn, I used to really like that stuff, now I'd probably forever associate it with her. "Oh, I'm so glad *you* could *come*." Even though Will wasn't looking at me, I still threw a "you've got to be kidding me" look his way. "I'm Fiona, but you can call me Fee. Please come in." She stepped just far back enough so that Will would have to touch her in the process of squeezing past. She stepped further back for me. How considerate.

She took us through to her shabby chic living room and indicated I should sit in an armchair. Will, however, was directed to sit on the couch, which he did. She plonked next to him close enough that their thighs touched, even though she had a metre of couch left on her other side. Will looked at me, both brows raised in what I assumed was alarm. I shrugged. There was nothing I could do about it. I felt sorry for him, though. Sexual harassment wasn't nice, no matter who was doing the harassing.

Will turned to the woman. "Do you mind sitting a bit over that way? I don't like strangers in my personal space. We endeavour to keep all our interviews professional. If we can't do that, we'll have to send someone else over later." My eyes widened. Wow, he actually said something. I smiled. Good on him.

*Fee's* mouth dropped open. She obviously wasn't used to her advances being rebuffed. Bad luck, lady. She scooted a few centimetres away from him, her movements stiff and slow with reluctance. At least now we could get started.

I had my pad and pen at the ready, and Will asked the first question. "Great. Now, when did you first realise something was missing or wasn't right?" He gave her a polite smile that said everything was forgiven, but it wasn't friendly enough that she'd invade his space again. Lucky for her, she'd acted on his request because I hadn't forgotten how to give small electric shocks. I smirked when I thought back to the fashion designer last month who couldn't keep her hands to herself. Yes, I was a tad evil, but no one was perfect.

She settled her hands in her lap and twisted one of her gold rings around her finger over and over. "Well, I was out yesterday afternoon. I got home around five thirty, and my front door was open."

"Was there any sign of forced entry?"

"No."

"And what was taken?"

*Twist, twist, twist.* "A little plush toy of a husky, three-hundred pounds—it's my emergency stash of money I keep in my bedside table—and Coco, my three-year-old husky."

"As in a live dog?" Will asked.

"Yes." Her lip quivered, and her eyes glistened. As annoying as she'd been, my heart went out to her. It looked like she lived here on her own, so her dog was likely her much-loved fur baby.

Will's voice became kinder. "Are you sure Coco didn't run away because the door was open?"

She shook her head. "No. Even though he's a big dog, he's timid and prefers to be inside. I do walk him, but only at the local park—he's used to it and doesn't play up too much. He can get rather nippy when he's scared, and the last thing I want is for him to bite another dog or person. He's gotten out twice before, and he just sat inside the front yard watching the world go by. They're expensive dogs. Dog theft is a thing, you know."

"Yes, we're aware. Do you have a photo of Coco we can add to our file? Is he microchipped?"

"Yes and yes. Hang on a minute." She stood and left the room. She returned shortly after with her phone. "I can send it to you. Do you have a mobile I can text to?"

I piped up. "I do." There was no worry she'd be trying to chat me up later if she had my number, but with Will, you never knew.

Her hopeful expression was replaced by disappointment. She turned from me and looked at Will. "I'd rather if I could text it directly to you, since you're in charge."

Will cleared his throat and shifted another centimetre away from her so he was squished against the arm of the couch. "No. Sending to my colleague is best. She coordinates everything for me."

I smiled. "If you're ready to put my number into your phone, we can get this done before we check out the door and where the things were missing from."

"Fine." Well, that was a tad ungrateful.

I gave her my number, and Will stood. "Oh, one more question. Have you had any tradesmen inside your home in the last few weeks?"

She bit her bottom lip as she thought. "My oven was on the blink two weeks ago. The guy from Miele came and fixed it for me. I've got his card if you need it."

"That would be great, thanks." Will smiled.

She went in the opposite direction to last time, then returned and handed Will the card. He gave me a nod. I stood, went to him, and took a screenshot of the card, which he then handed back to *Fee*.

Will got up. "We have to take a few photos, and then we'll be out of your hair."

She stood and smiled at Will. "No hurry. Would you like a cup of tea?"

"No thanks. We have quite a few houses to get to today. The burglar's been busy." He smiled and walked towards the front door. I followed, taking my lens cap off and turning my camera on. Will looked at me. "I'm just going to see if I can find any evidence. If you could photograph the scene?"

Hopefully he'd find the magic signature used to open the door, unless they were picking locks, which seemed to be the case in a few of the homes the other day. Only the tricky-to-open doors were opened with magic, and some, well, we had no idea how they'd even gotten in. And that was the first time I'd heard him ask that question—whether someone had been inside the past few weeks. They could've made a landing spot, but surely that would take too long and be ridiculously obvious, not to mention the power it would take to do that in lots of houses. I'd have to ask Will about it later.

I held the camera up. *Show me Coco leaving.* The front door was open, but it was dark both inside and out—Fiona obviously hadn't come home yet. The husky stood on the front porch, looking out at the front yard. I clicked off a shot from inside. I moved to the door and stood on the threshold. It was hard to make out, but there was definitely a person standing out on the footpath. And hang on, what was that? There was another dog, a small one standing between the person and Coco. Had they used a dog to lure the husky outside? This was getting weirder and weirder. I took another picture, then moved beyond the front porch, but things just became darker rather than clearer. I gave up and lowered the Nikon. Bright daylight was disconcerting. It didn't matter how often I used my talent, I was often discombobulated at the difference in environments. Even though I wasn't going anywhere when I looked through my camera lens, it was as if I'd time travelled.

I went back into the house and found Fiona's bedroom.

*Show me who stole the three hundred pounds*. Nothing. I sighed and turned the camera off. That was it for this house. I met Will outside. "I'm done."

"Did you get anything? I did. Same signature as before."

"Here." I handed him the camera. He scrolled through the pictures. "Hmm, interesting."

We made our way to the next house, and the next, and the next, until we'd seen eleven different homes. I climbed into the Range Rover and buckled my seat belt. "Gah, same old, same old information. The only thing I am kind of sure about is that the person we keep seeing outside is the same person in all the photos today. I don't think there's a gang."

"We can't be sure, though. There could be two people who are a similar size and height. They'd pretty much look the same in the dark."

"I s'pose." I sighed and looked out the window. "What if we never solve this case?"

He shrugged. "It's not the end of the world, but there will be a lot of unhappy people. The cash and jewellery taken are adding up. Not to mention how many people are missing their pets, although I do wonder how many just ran away."

"That little dog seemed to be waiting for the husky to come out."

"Yes, but it's possible the person wanted the dog out of the house so they didn't get attacked."

"They're a witch. Would it even matter?"

He grunted. And *I* was the forgetful one who had to be reminded about all the things witches were capable of. Ha!

Why was I even happy? It didn't make this any easier to figure out. I hated not knowing. At least people weren't dying. *Touch wood*. I touched the timber strip on Will's dash. He glanced at me. "What are you doing?"

"Satisfying my need to appease the superstition gods."

He laughed. "Okay. I don't know why I expected an answer that made sense. I really should know better."

"Yes, you should." I smirked.

The next location was ten minutes north. There were six houses to visit. We went through them in about an hour, and then we were done. We discovered about a third of all the places we'd visited had some kind of tradesman visit in the last few weeks, but none of them were from the same company or there for the same reason. It looked like that was a dead end. So how were they getting inside without magic and without opening doors? I wriggled my bottom and quietly screamed.

Will's brow furrowed. "What's wrong?"

"Frustrated, that's all. This is taking us a long time to get to the bottom of. Is there even a pattern with the types of houses or streets they're targeting? At this stage, we won't find out who it is until we catch them in the act."

"Stop stressing. That's pretty much impossible unless you can tell the future now. Do you know how many houses are in the UK?"

"Not exactly, but, yes, I know it's impossible, hence the frustration. I hate not figuring it out."

"Well, we have a bigger list of things for Imani to look for at the pawnshops, and we need to get all the pet pictures and chip details into the system so we can alert UK vets and animal shelters. Either these pets will turn up as strays, or maybe they've been sold, and we can trace them to their new owners. It's somewhere to start."

"True." Okay, that was better than nothing. A tiny piece of my despondency broke off and floated away. I waved to it.

Will glanced at me again. "I'm not even going to ask this time."

Wise man.

Instead of going home, Will drove to PIB headquarters. "Why are we here?" I asked as we passed security and drove through to the underground car park.

"We need to get that information into the system and see what comes up. I have some other stuff to do, but I figured you could take it all up to Liv and you guys could work on it together."

I grinned. I hadn't seen much of Liv lately. "Sounds good. I can handle that."

"I'm not sure how long I'll need to be here, so when you've finished, you can travel home. I'll drive home later." He parked the car and leaned over. The kiss he planted on my lips was sweet and too short. We couldn't kiss in front of everyone upstairs, so he was saying goodbye here.

We hopped in the lift. He pressed the button for the second floor, and I pressed number one—my favourite level because it held the cafeteria. Will smirked. "You can't go half a day without eating."

"So? I'm not a camel."

He grinned. "No, you're more like a bear preparing to hibernate for the winter, only we're going into summer."

"That wasn't beary nice." The lift dinged, almost but not quite drowning out Will's groan, and the doors opened. I stepped out and turned for one last pun. "You should apolargise." I grinned as the doors slid shut; then I giggled. I cracked myself up. Annoying Will was just a bonus.

I grabbed a coffee for me, tea for Liv, two cheese-and-ham croissants, and two blueberry muffins—they were disappointingly out of chocolate ones. I returned to the lift and went up to Liv's office, which was also Millicent's. Happily, they were both there. "Hey, ladies. Millicent, I didn't get anything for you, but you're welcome to pick something." I set it all on her table. I could always grab more food later.

"Nothing for me, thanks. I'm ducking home to feed Annabelle in a minute. I'll grab something then." She smiled.

"Are you sure?"

"Positive. I'll probably work from home this afternoon too. I want to get some training in with the girls." She winked. We obviously couldn't talk about anything here. Even though we usually had a bubble of silence activated, you never knew who could be listening and what spells they'd managed to invent to get around our protections. At least at James's or Angelica's there were strong wards around the properties, thanks to Robert. But at the PIB? We could be surrounded by double agents—agents who were loyal to Dana Piranha. We could never be too careful.

Liv spun her chair around and wheeled it to Millicent's table. "What did you bring me, oh awesome one?"

"The usual." I grabbed my coffee and took a sip, then sat.

"Smells divine." She looked up at Millicent. "Last chance to get in on the action."

She laughed. "Nope. I'm good. In fact, I might as well get going. I'll see you both later." She grabbed her bag and laptop, made her doorway, and walked through.

As we ate, I explained to Liv what Will wanted us to do. I drew on my magic and willed all the information onto a piece of paper. I wasn't skilled enough to magic it onto a memory stick or directly onto the computer. You needed a special spell that was compatible to computer language, whatever that meant. Two piles of paper appeared on Liv's desk. "There's a list of stuff we can give to Millicent and Imani to check up on, but the other information is about the missing pets. We need to send it to all the vets in the UK, make sure they get back to us if they see any. I've also got photos for each pet."

"Okay, but what about your *other* photographic evidence."

I shook my head. "There isn't much."

Her eyes widened. "Bummer."

"Yep."

We finished eating, and I sat at her desk. She worked on her desktop and passed me her laptop. I magicked the photos and documents into the system, which took all of one minute. Liv shook her head. "I still can't get over how easy you guys make everything. And, to think, I used to think scanners were impressive."

"Yeah, if only we didn't have to hide everything from the world. Everyone would have it so much easier." Why did people have to be so unpredictable? Yes, they might be scared if they knew what we could do, and that's where the problem lay. Instead of looking at all the positives, they'd kill first and ask questions later.

After the information was in the system, we could email every vet with all the details, which we did. She took one list, and I took the other. It would look spammy if we "sent all," so we did them individually, which was time-consuming. I wasn't quite sure of a spell to speed up the process, and I figured by the time I worked it out, I'd have done it all anyway. It only took us thirty minutes, so it wasn't too bad.

My phone dinged. I grabbed it out of my jacket pocket. James had sent a message. *Meeting at mine tonight. 7 pm.*

I replied, *Okay. I'll be there.* The contents of my stomach did a little flip, nervousness prodding my lunch. Were we going to send the rats into the factory tomorrow? I swallowed. What if something happened to Bagel or Cinnamon? As silly as it sounded, I'd grown attached to those two sweet creatures. If they died helping us, I'd be distraught.

I turned my phone around and showed Liv, although hers dinged as soon as I did. "You've probably got the same one." I wasn't going to elaborate. She looked at her phone and nodded.

"Right, now what?" I asked. We'd done what Will had

asked, and Liv probably had other work to get through. "Do you need my help with any of your stuff?"

"Um…" She looked at the ground, then back at me, her mouth silenced by guilt. It was easy to tell. She found it hard to say anything mean, and she was struggling to find any words, which was very un-Liv like.

I smiled. "Hey, it's fine. Top-secret stuff. I understand. It's not like I'm an agent, and even then, they don't share everything with everyone. I guess it means I have the afternoon off, and I can go home and nap. I'm still a bit tired from the other day." I held my arm up, indicating the tattoo.

She gave me an apologetic smile. "I'm sorry. I feel weird keeping secrets from you."

"Hey, don't worry. It's your job. Goodness knows I can't tell you everything either. So we're even." I grinned. "I'll see you later." I stood, slid my phone in my pocket, and grabbed my camera. With one last wave, I made my doorway and left.

# CHAPTER 9

After eating dinner by myself at home, I met everyone at my brother's place. The usual gang was there, and I sat between Imani and Will. Bagel and Cinnamon were on the table in their shoebox. Before explaining what was going to happen, James waited for them to emerge. These sentient beings were going to be given the choice of whether they wanted to do this or not. I was worried for their welfare, but I did hope they'd say yes. Guilt was at constant war with my desire to find out what happened to my parents, not to mention, I would love to have a normal life, where I could go where I wanted when I wanted. Okay, so normal was relative when you were a witch, but you know what I mean.

Bagel and Cinnamon slowly exited their safe house. As soon as Bagel saw me, she scurried across the table, claws scrabbling for purchase. When she reached the edge of the table, she leaped across and held fast to my jumper. "Hello, cutie. How have you been?" I stroked her back.

She squeaked. I looked across the table at Millicent. She smiled. "I'm going to be translator again, am I? I'll have to teach you how to talk to her."

My mouth dropped open as excitement sizzled through me. "Could I really learn how?"

"Yes. I'll give you a lesson after this. Anyway, Bagel said hello, and she's overjoyed to see you."

Well, that wasn't hard to come up with. I'd already figured that, since she'd run to me and thrown herself at my chest. Maybe I didn't need to learn how to magically speak to animals—they were pretty obvious when they wanted to be. I smiled down at her. "Well, I'm overjoyed to see you too." She made another little squeak, which I took for thanks.

James cleared his throat. "I'd like to start, if we could." Once he had everyone's attention, rats included, he began. "It's time to investigate the factory in Manchester. Tomorrow night." Adrenaline shot through me, warming my stomach and chest. This was it, the next step in our search for answers. "I've had surveillance on the factory to see who comes in and out and when. Everyone is gone by 7:00 p.m., and two security guys are patrolling from seven until six the next morning, when the first workers arrive. The security guys are witches." I put up my hand. "Yes, Lily?"

"I'm not questioning your decisions, but I just need to know for my own peace of mind."

"Yes?" James raised a brow. Okay, so he assumed I was about to question his decisions. Maybe I shouldn't have led with anything, just came straight out and asked, but that would've been a bit blunt.

"Who was doing the surveillance? Can we trust them? Even if you didn't say why, surely word could get back to Dana's people in the PIB?"

He shook his head. "I should've known you'd have to ask. The answer is yes; we can totally trust them. Robert's helped me develop drones that look like birds. They've been constructed with magic, but they operate just like any drone would—with a manual controller. They've been sitting in trees that overlook the premises. I occasionally send them for a flyover—they have a quiet stealth mode."

"Couldn't we have just used something like that to look inside?"

"No. Even though they're quiet, they're not dead silent, and the noise would be magnified in a confined space. And if someone caught one, they'd quickly work out what they are. Then we'd be in trouble, obviously."

"Fair enough." At least he answered me without getting angry or insulting, which was a massive step up from dealing with Angelica. I knew she cared about me, but she was one hard person to please. I supposed she just had really, really high standards because, in her line of work, mediocrity got people killed. How many agent deaths did she feel responsible for? I shook my head to stop my line of thinking. Sending myself into a downward spiral wouldn't help anyone, not to mention, I should be paying attention.

"Now, in terms of who's going. We don't need a huge contingent—this is an exploratory fact-finding mission to help us next time. Millicent will go, of course, because she needs to stay in contact with her charges." He glanced at Bagel, who had climbed onto my shoulder, and Cinnamon, who sat on the table in front of Millicent. "As much as I want to go, if I can avoid both Millicent and I being in danger at the same time, I will—we have someone else to think about, and God forbid she became an orphan."

"Don't say that! You guys are going to be around for years to come." My outburst had materialised before I could even think about what was spewing out of my mouth. Everyone looked at me, but no one said the obvious: James and I were orphans. That dreadful outcome was possible.

James cleared his throat. "I'm sending Will with Millicent. That's it. Too many witches hanging around might draw suspicion, although I'm trusting you two to stay out of sight." He looked at his wife, then Will. They both nodded.

Will gave James a lopsided smile. "In case you hadn't noticed, we're trained professionals."

James laughed. "That you are. Sorry, but it's hard not to let this get to me. This is… personal." My brother's intense gaze met mine. A maelstrom of emotions warred in his eyes: sadness, loss, anger, fear.

I blinked back tears. "It's okay, James. We're going to succeed. No one is going to die because of this. I won't let it happen." I hoped he realised I was offering my power to him if he needed it. We'd healed Ma'am and Beren before, together. Will knew my secret too—I'd lent him my power when we needed to bring Angelica back to life. It was a secret that couldn't get out, though. I was the first witch in hundreds of years who could lend my power to someone else, or take it if I so chose. This talent made me dangerous, and if anyone outside our circle found out, it would make me a target for more than RP. Whatever it took, though, I was up for it.

"Thanks, sis." His demeanour changed as he shed the negativity. "Right, so Bagel and Cinnamon are going to be wearing the tiny cameras, which also have audio. Everything will be streamed back to a recording device Millicent will be carrying. We'll get the lay of the land and a better idea as to where the security cameras are and how often the security guards check inside and where they go. Any extra information the rats may come across will be a bonus. Unfortunately, we're going to have to get in there ourselves at some point and have a look around, but we'll need to know how to disable their security systems—both magical and non."

"What time do you want me here?" asked Will. "I'll travel with Millicent."

"Be here at seven. The closest landing spot is five minutes' walk. You can check things out, and as soon as the best window for releasing the rats presents itself, they can run in. I have a floor plan of the place you can check over when we're done here. There are four possible entry points for our little friends." He looked at Bagel and smiled. "Oh, that reminds me, are you both happy to undertake this mission?" He swung his gaze around to Cinnamon. She nodded. Liv sucked in a breath. I shook my head slowly, in awe. I knew they understood, I *knew*, but seeing them respond in such a human way blew my tiny mind. Bagel squeaked—she really was the more vocal of both rats. I guessed we suited each other.

Millicent nodded. "They both say yes, but there is a condition."

James made sure he kept his serious face because, honestly, negotiating with rats was comical. When I was a kid, hell, even one year ago, the last thing that would have ever crossed my mind was that one day I'd be talking to rats. Go figure. "Yes?"

"When we have no use for their skills, they want to live with us, and if there are times we can't look after them, they want to live with Lily."

I grinned. That was beyond adorable. Angelica might not approve, but bad luck. If they needed to live with us, they could. Besides, if worst came to worst, I could always get a loan and buy my own place or rent somewhere else. The last few months had been lucrative. The PIB paid better than a lot of photography jobs, and I'd had consistent work—not that I'd wanted it, but….

James rubbed his forehead. "Um, is that healthy with the baby and everything?"

Millicent raised a brow. "They don't take much to look after. When have you had to do anything for them?"

He looked chagrined. "Um… never?"

"That's right, *darling*. Besides, we're witches. When is any kind of housework a chore?" She had him there.

He put his hands up in surrender. "Okay, okay, it's a deal."

Bagel tapped me on the cheek. I turned to look at her and went cross-eyed. Whoa, that was way too close. But I got the gist. "I promise to look after both of you if for any reason Millicent and James can't. I've got your backs." Bagel touched her nose to mine. I was pretty sure that meant "yay."

After a moment, Millicent said, "Right, they're happy with that. Now, what are the rest of the details?"

As James outlined what was coming next, I stroked Bagel's back. *Mum and Dad, we're getting there. Not long now.*

I crossed my fingers that tomorrow night would go without a hitch.

# CHAPTER 10

The next day was mostly a non-event, which was torture. Other than travelling to the PIB compound and doing a few laps of the vast outdoor area to burn off some nervous energy, I spent my time reading, wandering Angelica's house, and biting my fingernails, until three o'clock, when Will came home.

"Hey! You're not supposed to be here. Is work quiet?" I asked from my favourite armchair next to the fire.

"Never quiet. I'm here because we've had a call from a vet."

I closed the cover on my iPad and sat up straighter. "What happened?"

"One of the missing animals was brought in this afternoon."

I wrinkled my forehead. Will's news should've made his

face happier, but the look he sported was anything but. "And?"

"It was dead. Mrs Horsham's black-and-white cat."

"Oh." My shoulders sagged. That poor cat. "How did it die? Has anyone told Mrs Horsham? As much as I didn't really like her, she's going to be devastated. That's so sad."

"There were no obvious signs of injury, so it wasn't hit by a car. I'm going to collect the body now, run it to the PIB for a once over; then we'll take Mervin to Mrs Horsham."

"Maybe he died of natural causes? I mean, how do you know he was stolen? He probably just wandered off like we originally thought." The cat dying could've easily been a coincidence.

"Because Mervin was found ten miles from home. I'm infinitely sure cats don't wander quite that far. I want to check his paws too. There'd be telltale signs if he walked all that way. I'm more interested to see if there's a magic signature anywhere. He could've been killed by magic. So, you interested in coming to collect him? I figured you'd want to get out." His smile was a little too… hopeful.

"You know me too well." I cocked my head to the side. "Hang on a minute. You want me to break the news about Merv's demise to Mrs Horsham, don't you?"

His smile was genuine this time. "And you know *me* too well. I'm terrible with stuff like that. My cranky face gets in the way. I don't know how to do gentle and kind with people I don't know. Please?" He stepped up to me and cupped my cheek in his hand.

I rolled my eyes. "All right. All right. Stop with the

begging. It doesn't suit you." I stood and magicked my iPad to my room.

"Thank you!" He threw his arms around me, giving me a huge hug. "This hug is for real. It's me saying I appreciate it. I do. Really."

"Yeah, yeah, I know. If I didn't think so, I would've said no. Come on, then. Let's get this over with." I drew on my magic, clicking my fingers for fun. My PIB suit replaced my tracksuit, and I grabbed my camera, just in case. Will sent me the coordinates, and I stuck them on my doorway.

I arrived in the usual, nondescript public toilet. I stepped outside to a small park. A library sat across the road and near that a three-storey block of units. Will emerged from the toilet block. I turned to him. "Where are we?"

"Caterham."

"Okay. Glad I asked." I had no idea where most things in the UK were—I knew London, Westerham, a couple of suburbs nearby, Dover, and Brighton. Okay, so I'd been more places than I'd thought, but Caterham rang no bells, and I had nothing to reference it off, so it was useless information. Although, I supposed if anyone said anything about Caterham, I could say I'd been.

Will pulled his phone out and brought up Google Maps. He looked at it, then at our surroundings. He pointed. "We need to walk along that road for about three minutes."

"Nice and easy, but then we have to walk back here with a dead body."

"It's not like it's a human body, Lily. It'll be lucky to weigh five kilos."

"It's still dead, and it's a body. I rest my case."

He shook his head and set off. Sure enough, we soon arrived at a two-storey house-like structure. It was a 1920s building that would've been a grand home in its early days. Now it contained Caterham Vet and Animal Hospital. Will opened the door for me. Such a gentleman. I let him take the lead once we were inside the waiting room. Seven of the ten chairs were occupied. One mother sat in between two young children. A depressed-looking beagle lay at her feet. An old couple had a black cat in a cage. A young man, muscles bulging through his long-sleeve T-shirt, cradled a Yorkshire terrier in his lap, and an old man held the leash of an overweight Labrador. Yep, it was a normal day at the vet.

Will approached the middle-aged woman at the counter. "I'm here about a black-and-white cat called Mervin."

"Oh, yes. Hang on a moment." She turned and disappeared down a tiled corridor. She returned with a young woman in green scrubs—obviously the vet.

"I'm Lauren Folks. You must be Agent Blakesley?"

"Yes, and this is my colleague, Ms Bianchi."

"Hi," I said, feeling awkward. Was I fraud, turning up to these investigations? I had the suit, but I wasn't an agent. I always felt like I was lying to people in these situations, like, if they knew I was just a photographer, would they be upset?

"Please come this way." Lauren turned and went back down the hallway.

A dog barked in one of the rooms we passed. Lauren opened the door to her right. "Please come in." The room was your average vet-consultation room with a sink, shelves, and a stainless-steel trolley examination table. There was a second door. Lauren went to it. "Just a moment, and I'll grab the body."

As soon as she left, I turned to Will. "I told you it was a body!"

He rolled his eyes. "Yes, and I didn't argue with you. I just pointed out that it's a small body that isn't human, so not worth panicking about."

"I wasn't panicking. I just don't like handling dead things."

He looked at me like I was an idiot. "Lily, do you or do you not cook meat?"

"Yeah, yeah, but it's already cut up in neat little portions with inoffensive names like cutlet, scotch fillet, rump, and mince." Hmm, maybe mince was a little on the violent side. "And those cuts of meat certainly aren't cute, cumbersome, or floppy."

Will opened his mouth to say something, but *unfortunately*, Lauren returned carrying a black plastic bag filled with something floppy and dead. I sighed. Poor Mervin. She laid him gently on the trolley. "There's no sign of trauma causing death. He appeared to have died a natural death, but since we aren't going to do an autopsy, it's just a guess. He could have been poisoned. He's not an old cat, so there's no reason he should have just dropped dead. There was one thing, which is what made me second guess reporting his death to your office. He doesn't have a council microchip, and I didn't know if he was the cat you were after, but after comparing him to the photo on file, I thought it was worth a call. There were no obvious incisions for the removal of the microchip, but someone's removed it. Once you told us the cat's name and address, I checked our database, and he was definitely registered. Anyway, I'll leave you to figure out the why of that."

Will wrinkled his forehead. Well, that was a development. "Thanks so much for contacting our agency so quickly. As soon as we're done with Mervin, we'll inform his owner and return him, which should all be by tomorrow. Oh, and where was he found?"

"Hang on." She opened a drawer and took out a sheet of paper. "Burntwood Lane, under some bushes. It's a popular walking trail—it's not in the woods, but it has good footpaths." Hmm, sounded lovely if you liked walking alongside the road. Yeah, nah.

"Thanks again. We appreciate your help." Will gave her a nod. He scooped up Mervin, and then we said goodbye and left.

Outside, Will brought up his map again. "Hmm, looks like the leafy part of Burntwood Lane is only about a mile from the toilets. Feel like a walk and a chance for some photography?"

"Why not? I have nothing else to do this afternoon." Keeping busy today was my goal. I did not want to dwell on what was happening tonight.

As we walked, I pretended Will was carrying a bag full of plastic bags. "Will?"

"Yes?"

"Maybe you should magic that to the PIB when we get

to the toilets, you know, before we go to the other place. It would be easier on both of us."

He chuckled. "You're one funny woman, Lily. You think nothing of striking people down with lightning bolts, but you're squeamish about a dead cat."

I shrugged. "This is going to sound really, really horrible, but maybe I like animals more than I do a lot of people? Merv didn't have a choice about what happened to him—he didn't break a law or set out to hurt anyone. And for the record, I don't enjoy killing people. In fact, I'm horrified every time."

"Yet, you keep doing it." He shook his head, a lopsided smile on his face. "As far as Merv not being malicious in killing things, I would think a few skinks, mice, and birds would beg to differ."

The toilet block was up ahead, thankfully. This wasn't the most fun conversation I'd ever had. "Yes, but that's just Merv working on instinct, keeping his hunting skills up to date in case he actually needed to feed himself. I'm not saying I like that cats kill other animals, but it's not malicious. Humans, on the other hand…."

"I guess I can't argue with you there." He stopped at the toilets. "Wait here." He ducked inside. His magic feathered my scalp, and then he returned, sans Merv. We followed his phone's directions to Burntwood Lane.

The narrow street had a pleasantly level footpath that ran alongside a narrow street. Eventually we came to an area that had shrubbery on the other side. Shrubbery was a weird word, but it did suit the idea of lots of tightly packed leaves all hanging together. I guessed you could say those plants were shrubbing around. Or maybe not. Was it bad that I found myself annoying sometimes?

Will halted. "Time to get the camera out. This looks like the spot."

"There might be more spots up ahead."

"Well, we'll look at those if this one doesn't pan out. I don't mean to sound like Ma'am, but where's your brain this afternoon, Lily?"

I gazed at the shrubs. "Probably in there, hiding." I turned my camera on and took the lens cap off. There was nowhere to stand on the other side of the road, so we stayed where we were. It was pretty close anyway, and it was the kind of shot where I wanted to see the bigger picture, both figuratively and literally.

"Show me who dumped Mervin's body here." Aaaaaaand, it was dark. The streetlight a few metres away didn't give me much to go on. Whoever was laying his body on the ground was crouched and in shadow. I took a photo and lowered the camera. I walked along the footpath a bit before checking the road for cars and crossing to where there was another path. I pointed my camera towards the shrubs and repeated my question. The person appeared again. I zoomed in and shot a couple more photos. I crossed the road back to Will and showed him the near-useless pictures.

"At least we've confirmed he didn't die of natural causes. But why kill him? They could've just dropped him at the end of his street, and he would've found his own way home, no one the wiser."

"People are mean. Remember?"

He shook his head. "I'm in the business of finding out why. Knowing why brings us to motivation, which can be both a clue and is valuable in court. If we can come up with some scenarios of the why, it will bring us closer to who is doing it. Why did they kill the cat? They had no reason to, and, in fact, they've left a clue by killing him and dumping his body. They might have thought no one would find Mervin, but that was an oversight."

"Well, they certainly thought they'd be safe, removing his microchip first. Why didn't they bury him in their yard?"

"Maybe they don't have a yard? Anyway, we have a lot of questions, and none of them are getting answered while we stand here. I want to get back to headquarters and talk to Beren. If anyone can get to the bottom of the cat's death, it's him, and we don't want to wait. The longer we take, the more faded the magic signature will be and any evidence of spells. Come on. Let's go."

BACK AT HEADQUARTERS, WILL RUSHED OFF TO THE AUTOPSY room to meet Beren, and I ambled down to the cafeteria. I didn't feel like being by myself at home, so I magicked my iPad to myself and read—I had checked with Liv in case she needed my help, but the answer was no.

After a couple of hours—almost a whole book, three

cappuccinos, a toasted cheese-and-tomato sandwich, and a chocolate muffin—my phone dinged. Will. Finally. I magicked my iPad back home and threw my rubbish in the bin, then headed to Will's office for a small meeting. At least I had clearance for magicking things back and forth. Agents could, too, but any witch guests would've been blocked by one of the security spells. It wouldn't do to have a criminal or stranger turning up, getting cleared through security, then magicking a weapon to themselves.

I knocked but didn't wait for an answer before opening the door to his little waiting room. Beren's voice filtered out from Will's office. I went to the open door and poked my head in. "Hey."

Will grinned. "Come in and have a seat. We've got some news." Ooh, news. I liked news, as long as it helped us get where we wanted.

James was also in attendance. "Hey, Lily."

I smiled in reply as I sat next to Beren. James was on a chair on the other side of him, and Will sat across from us. There wasn't much social chit-chat since this was an ongoing investigation, and we were at work. Not that the guys weren't friendly, but everyone was in work mode, so I took their cue and stayed quiet. Big of me, I know.

Will sat back in his leather office chair and folded his arms in a relaxed manner. "I'll let you do the honours, B, since you're the one who did the autopsy."

"Okay, thanks." He stood and went around to Will's side of the desk and stood facing James and me. He smiled. "We found more than I thought we would. The microchip had been removed with magic, and the cat's heart had been stopped with magic. I found a magic signature on the body, and both spells were still there—faint but enough to decipher. I've put all that into our system. It's the same signature Will found at all the previous locations, so we can surmise that we're dealing with one witch. How that witch is carrying out these crimes so fast is another matter. But at this stage, we're hunting one perpetrator."

James leaned forward and rested his forearms on the table. "That makes things simpler. What else have you got?"

"Not much. I did look at the contents of Mervin's stomach, and I've given them to the lab. If he's eaten cat food, we might be able to at least find out what type. It's a long shot, but if it matches what the criminal has at home, it's just another evidency mark against his or her name in court."

James raised his brow. "Did you just say 'evidency?'"

Beren shrugged. "Yes. Is that a problem?"

"It's not a real word." My brother turned to look at me. "It's your bad influence."

Beren grinned. "She's a blooming good influence if you ask me. I enjoy making up words, and evidency just fit. You knew what I meant, didn't you?"

James sighed, and his answer took a beat too long. He obviously didn't want to make the admission. "Yes, fine."

"I rest my case." Beren leaned across the table towards me and held his hand up for a high five. I stood and slapped it.

"Nice work, B. I heartily approve of your efforts."

"Why, thank you, Miss Bianchi."

James rolled his eyes, and Will grinned. He unfolded his arms and sat up straight. "Sorry to be a party pooper, but the fun's over. The burglar strikes at night, so we'll have more cases to investigate tomorrow, no doubt. The evidence we have so far isn't enough to lead us in any direction, so we'll just have to hope something else turns up."

James looked at me, then Will. "There's the little matter of who's going to tell Mrs Horsham about Mervin?"

"I thought we could give that assignment to Imani, if she's not too busy." I blinked. Will had told me earlier he'd wanted me to do it. Looked like he'd changed his mind, or maybe he was seeing if he could get away with us not doing it.

"Way to avoid the hard stuff, mate. The answer would be no. She's busy, and I think it's better if someone familiar to Mrs Horsham conveys the news. I'm sure I can trust you and Lily to do the job in a compassionate manner." Wow, James was tough when he needed to be. I knew him though, and this was done out of necessity. Someone had to do it, and why not us? No one liked to tell someone their loved one had died. My heart went out to all the police who'd had to make that visit. Yes, we were only talking about a cat, but some people loved their pets as if they were their children, so it was still going to be miserable.

I nodded because I'd already come to terms with the assignment earlier. "We'll do it, and we'll do it as nicely as possible. I'll even try not to cry." My poker face might be bad, but me trying not to cry in an emotional situation was even worse. Maybe there was a spell I could use to stop everything gushing to the surface at the wrong moment?

Will gave me a sympathetic look. "It's okay, Lily. I'll tell her. You just come with me and provide moral support."

"I can do that. But are you sure? Earlier you—"

He shook his head. "Nope, it's fine. You're not even an agent. It was unfair of me to ask you." Ah, so that was his change of heart.

James raised a brow. "You already asked her?"

"Yeah, but I thought better of it just now. Imani is good at this stuff with all her spiritual hocus pocus."

I laughed. "You're calling witch stuff hocus pocus?"

"No, just the spiritual stuff she believes in. We may all be witches, but we still have our own belief systems. We all know about the river from which all magic is drawn, but who put it there in the first place? Was it whoever discovered magic or a powerful being? Or was it nature or the mysterious forces beyond our reality? Imani believes in an earth mother, so to speak. Surely you've heard her talk about it before?"

"Yep, and I agree—she's much nicer than we are."

Beren's forehead crinkled. "We are talking about the same Imani, aren't we?" He laughed. "She's one tough nut, but I know what you mean. I've seen her be particularly nurturing when she needs to be."

"I have nothing bad to say about her. She's promised to protect me to the death. To be honest, no other friend has ever offered that before. I, in turn, will never hear a bad word said about her." I smiled. I knew they weren't being mean—it was true; she was scary to most people. She didn't take crap, and she wasn't afraid to call you out. I was glad she was on my side.

James stood. "This is all wasting time. You lot are hopeless. Give you a minute to chat and you take ten. Just make sure you're nice to Mrs Horsham. Don't tell her about the autopsy. Beren's magicked it so Mervin has not a scar on him. You can tell her where he was found and that we're following it up. Okay?"

"Yes, Sir," said Will.

"See you tonight." James left the normal way… well, the normal way for non-witches. Gah, I'd happily forgotten about tonight. Not that I was doing anything. I'd just be waiting at James's on pins and needles till Will and Millicent got back. I was looking after Annabelle so James wouldn't be distracted in case he had to travel to the scene urgently. I smiled. My niece had that effect on me. Happiness.

"I'll see you guys tomorrow. I've got stuff to catch up on." Beren stood and made a doorway. "Bye." He disappeared.

Will stood. "Looks like it's just you and me, kid."

I grinned. "Just the way it should be."

He smiled. "Always."

We walked out of his office and to the lift. The doors opened, and Will stood aside. "After you." I hopped in. He followed and pressed B. His sad eyes met mine. "Time for us to ruin someone's day."

Bummer.

# CHAPTER 11

Settled comfortably into James and Millicent's couch, I held the bottle of breastmilk to Annabelle's mouth, and she sucked hungrily, her hands resting on the bottle. She was still too young to be doing much else, but it was fine—she was cute enough that it didn't matter. We could all stare at her for hours and be happy anyway.

"Hey, gorgeous baby. What do you think is happening at the factory? Do you think Cinnamon and Bagel are okay?" She ignored me. Babies. Sigh. Not the best conversationalists.

To avoid any distractions, James was in his study, watching the images the rats picked up as they wandered through the factory. Will and Millicent could also watch from Millicent's phone. A two-way voice thing was in each rat's ear so Millicent could whisper instructions. James had been in his study for the past thirty-five minutes, and each minute had felt like an hour. At least if he was in there, it meant nothing horrible was happening. If the situation took a dive, either Will and Millicent would end up here, or James would let me know he was leaving.

Once the bottle was empty, I put a white cloth nappy on my shoulder and burped Annabelle.

I hated waiting.

What if RP discovered our intrusion? What if they killed the rats or went after Will and Millicent? I sighed heavily. Annabelle took that moment to regurgitate some of her dinner onto me. "Good girl. Actually, you aren't a good girl. Why do we praise you little people when you vomit? No one's ever been happy when I've vomited. I remember one time when I was thirteen and I had a bad case of gast—"

James hurried into the room. "Lily, they're done."

"Oh my God, really?" I wanted to jump up and do something, but I still had Annabelle, and anyway, what the hell was I going to do? "Are they out and safe?"

He smiled, relief in his eyes. "Yes. They're on their way to the toilets, and then they'll come back here."

I couldn't help but giggle. "It's not every day you hear that statement."

He grinned. "I know, right?"

"I've never really asked, which is weird when I think about it, but how did you find out you were a witch? Did you take ages to adjust? And how come you never told me?" How was it I was only getting around to asking this now? I knew. I hadn't stopped since I'd come here. It was one thing after another, and if I'd ever thought to ask, it had always slipped my mind by the time I'd had time to ask.

He sat next to me and held his arms out towards me. "Here, I think she's done burping." I gave her a kiss on the forehead and handed her over. Then I took the gross nappy off my shoulder and magicked it into their washing machine. The benefits of magic. There weren't really any downsides when you thought about it.

"So?"

"I had a visit on my twenty-second birthday. My magic came in a bit early. I was beyond frustrated that day. My phone refused to turn on, and every time I sat down to watch the cricket, the reception went berko. I'd just thrown the remote across the room—" My mouth dropped open. I'd hardly ever seen James lose his temper like that. Then I laughed. He laughed too and shook his head. "I know, right? Anyway, I'd just thrown the remote when someone rang the doorbell. I answered it, and it was this snobby-looking woman with an English accent and tight bun, not a hair out of place."

"Angelica!"

"That's right."

I frowned, melancholy stealing my breath. I took a moment to swallow and breathe. "You left five days later." I'd never forget it. He'd driven to the airport—he'd hated my driving, not that there was anything wrong with it—and when he'd got his stuff out, I'd given him a huge hug and wished him well through my tears, then jumped into the front seat. I didn't try and stop him because he'd sacrificed a lot to look after me when our parents disappeared. The least I could do was let him have his awesome holiday, or so I'd thought that's what it was.

"Yep. Angelica explained about Mum and Dad's disappearance, how Mum used to work for the PIB. As soon as I got over the shock and disbelief, I agreed to join. But it took me a few months to adapt to being a witch. I mean, what the hell, right? Witches—what a crazy notion."

"Yet, here we are."

Sorrow and regret leeched from his gaze. "I'm sorry I had to leave, and I'm sorry I couldn't tell you. I mean, would you have believed me? Plus, I was suddenly a member of a secretive organisation, and I didn't want to get you into trouble or put you in danger. I knew that whoever took our parents could pose a risk to either of us, so I pretended I was having fun living and working here. I mean, I was having some fun…." He cringed as if he'd said something wrong.

I shook my head. "It's fine, James. You're allowed to be happy—you were allowed. I was angry and upset when you left, but you deserved to be free and live your life. You gave up so much for me. I never held it against you. Promise."

His exhale brought relief to his face. His talent was telling whether someone was lying, and I knew he knew that I wasn't having him on. "Thanks, Lily. I always worried, you know? I felt like you might never forgive me."

"Don't be ridiculous! Everyone is entitled to their life, and even though I always missed you, I got on with my life too. I was actually happy… that is, until my coffee machine broke and"—I affected Ma'am's accent—"*Angelica Constance DuPree, but you can call me Ma'am* showed up at my door." We both had a chuckle.

"You're quite good at that."

"Thanks." I smiled.

The sound of the reception-room door opening filtered through to us. Millicent was saying, "I know…." I jumped up and ran. I couldn't wait to find out what had happened, and I wouldn't believe everyone was fine until I saw for myself.

I came across them in the vestibule. Millicent was holding a shoebox. I stared at it. "Are they okay?" She smiled and lifted the lid. I peered in. Two furry, pointy faces stared up at me. "Yay! Look at you two cuties. I'm so glad you're okay."

Bagel looked at Millicent and squeaked. Millicent laughed. "She says of course they're fine. She also asked if you were always such a worrier?"

I laughed. "Are you sure she didn't say warrior? I mean, it would be an easy mistake to make."

Millicent rolled her eyes. "Where's my baby?"

I jerked my head towards the living area. "Just had a bottle and burp. James is giving her a cuddle." Millicent hurried out.

I turned to Will and gave him a huge hug. "How was it? Did you get everything you needed? Were they none the wiser?"

"All will be revealed in a moment. Why don't we do all this sitting down? I've just been standing outside in the cold, and I wouldn't mind a hot chocolate." I took his hand and dragged him to the living room, where he sat on a large armchair. He grabbed my waist and pulled me to sit on his lap. There were worse places I could sit. Happiness was where you found it… or maybe where you found yourself. I giggled. "What's so funny?"

"Ah, nothing. As in, you probably wouldn't find it funny, so don't worry."

"I'm inclined to believe you." His magic tingled my scalp. The rich fragrance of hot chocolate wove its magic around me.

"Mmm, that smells good."

He took a sip. "That's because it is. Mmmmm."

I licked my lips. "Are you going to offer me any?"

He looked at me, surprise on his face… feigned surprise because he was Ma'am's prize student when it came to poker faces. "What will you do for me if I make you one?"

"I won't make any stupid jokes for twenty-four hours."

"Make it thirty-six, and you have a deal."

I pulled a face. "Thirty-six? I don't know if I'm capable."

"Well, then, no hot chocolate for you."

Bagel squeaked. I looked down. She jumped on Will's shoe, then grabbed onto his black jeans. She climbed up his leg and onto my shoulder. From there, she put her little nose in his face and squeaked up a storm. I laughed. Ooh, he was getting a telling off and a half. Millicent laughed too, then translated. "Oh my God. You're in big trouble, Will. Bagel said that if you don't make Lily a hot chocolate, she's going to get me to magic her to your place and leave a little present in your shoes when you least expect it."

I held my hand up in front of Bagel. "High-five me, Bagel, baby." She touched her tiny paw into the middle of my palm.

Will rolled his eyes. "All you women ganging up on me isn't fair. Hey, James, are you going to help a brother?"

He laughed. "Count me out. I'm surrounded by girls in this house. I have to watch myself." He winked. "Besides, haven't you learnt anything by now?"

"Yeah, yeah, fine." His mouth quirked up on one corner into a half-grin. His dimple, the one that melted my insides, made an appearance. "You ready?" he asked.

I held out my hands, ready to receive the cup. His magic feathered the back of my neck, and a mug appeared in my hands. I quickly grabbed the handle and let go with my other hand—it was hot. Which, I supposed, was to be expected. I inhaled the chocolatey scent, then took a sip. "Mmmmm, this is good. Thank you, sweetie."

"Oh, it's sweetie now, is it?" He shook his head.

"Okay, now that the children have their hot chocolate, can you give us a recap, Mill?" James asked.

Millicent smirked. "I certainly can. So, everything went as planned. Will and I were able to stay a safe distance from the factory, and Bagel and Cinnamon did an exceptional job. Thank you, ladies." Bagel squeaked from her perch on my shoulder, and Cinnamon poked her head out of the lidless shoebox that Millicent had placed on the couch. "As I'm sure you saw from the video link, we've mapped the interior." Well, I hadn't seen anything. I'd have to ask to see it later. "We know where every camera, door, wall, piece of equipment, and office are. It was pretty much what you'd expect of a factory. There was one interesting find we didn't expect."

"Was that the trap door?" James asked.

"Yes. We have no idea what, if anything, is down there, but we've added it to our floor plan, and we'll make sure to investigate when we go in. There was a deadlock on it, and a surveillance camera pointing at it, so we can assume something important is behind that door. I think the day we get in, we need to have as many on the ground as we can, get in out within ten minutes if possible, before they find out we're in there."

Will magicked his empty cup away. "I had a look with my other sight, and there are magical protections on the place. I've worked out how to disable the ones on the outside, but I don't know what they've got inside. Although, they may have nothing. Their external shield is pretty good considering how big a building they're protecting."

"I agree about getting in and out quickly, but the more witches we get in there, the more likely those guards will feel the magic. And once we're found out, I wouldn't be surprised if we found ourselves in a showdown. We're dealing with the witch equivalent of the Mafia in a way. Whatever RP are working towards, it's illegal, and we've already seen that they're happy to kill. I don't like that Dana's let them in on our trade secrets, either. Whatever

PIB protocol we use, they might expect it. We're going to have to plan this to the nanosecond."

Could witches measure time in nanoseconds? I would imagine by the time your witch timepiece has counted the nanosecond, you're already way past it. Gah, I was my own worst enemy. That was such a waste of energy to think about, and it made my brain hurt. It was too late to be thinking of science things, let alone ones that didn't matter. Bagel patted my cheek, as if to say, there, there, stop thinking if it hurts. My body shook with silent laughter. She was so adorable.

Will had witnessed the exchange, and he narrowed his eyes. "Look at you two getting chummy. Are you having private jokes now?" Bagel squeaked out what was probably a laugh, and so did I. Will shook his head. "I see myself becoming obsolete in this equation."

I stroked his cheek with my palm, his five o'clock shadow rough against my skin. "It's okay. I still love you. I have enough room in my heart for all of you." I gave Bagel a gentle pat. I was kind of joking but kind of not. The little animal was fast becoming one of my favourite "people."

James looked at us. "You're turning this into a circus, guys. Come on."

I gave him an apologetic look. "I'm sorry. My mind wandered, as it does. Besides, it sounds like you've said all there is to say until we meet to actually plan this thing."

James frowned at Will, as if blaming him. Will shrugged. "Don't blame me, mate. She's *your* sister."

James sighed and looked at Millicent. She gave him a

gentle smile. "I think she's right, James. Why don't we call it a night and meet again another day, with everyone? You can play the video, and we'll all nut it out together."

"Okay. I give up." He looked at Will. "I'll be in touch about a date and time."

"Sounds good to me." Will nudged me so I'd get off his lap.

I stood, magicked my cup away, and gently placed Bagel in her shoebox. "Goodnight, sweet little rat." I kissed my niece's forehead and gave Millicent, then James quick hugs. "See you tomorrow." As Will stood, I made my doorway and stepped through to our reception room.

I unlocked the door and entered the hall, Will right behind me. A voice called out from the living area, "Lily, is that you?" Angelica was home.

"Yes, and Will." I went through. She was sitting on one of the armchairs in front of the cold fireplace. It was a bit nippy. The British and their disregard of the cold was one thing I didn't think I'd ever get used to. I sat in the other armchair. "How are you?" We hadn't seen much of her lately. She'd likely been avoiding us because she didn't want to know what we were up to when it came to RP. I had no idea what was going on with her, but whatever it was, it couldn't be good. And as funny as it sounded, I missed her. She might be a bit of a grump, but she had a good heart, and you always knew where you stood, especially if it was on her toes. I smiled at the thought.

She put her paperback down. Angelica had worked hard on not much sleep for the entire time I'd known her, yet she never looked tired. Tonight, dark circles framed the under-side of her eyes, and the vibrant energy inside them was gone. "I'm fine, dear. How are you? And please don't tell me everything you've been up to."

Will had quietly come in and sat on the arm of my chair. "We're good, Angelica. Busy with work and… other things. How's everything at work?" Will was brave, asking that question.

Her smile was tight. "Challenging." She stood and folded her arms, pinning the book in front of her chest protectively. This was not an Angelica I knew. What the hell was going on? She gave Will a sad look that was quickly devoured by her poker face. She would never accidentally reveal herself. Whatever it was, she wanted Will to know. "Don't worry about me. I'll be fine. You know, I was thinking about that case you solved, those suicides at Dover. You two did a great job. You work well together. In fact, the whole team we've built is just what Lily will need later." Will and I shared a worried look before giving her our attention again. "I'm going to bed. Whatever happens, I'll be fine. I want you both to know. And I will never ever abandon you." She turned and left, her steady footsteps disappearing up the stairs.

"Crap. What was that about?"

Will stood and stared after her. "I don't know, but I don't think we're supposed to ask. Just don't forget what she said. Okay? And definitely don't tell anyone about this."

"Okay." I stood and slid my arms around his waist. Something wasn't right, in a very big way. But if Angelica was her usual tight-lipped self, we wouldn't know what it was until it was fixed, or…. We were getting closer to finding out about my parents—we couldn't lose her now. Was she sick? Fear clogged my throat. I had to swallow before I could talk. "She's not sick, is she?"

"No. I wouldn't think so. Besides, Beren could probably heal anything."

"Oh, yeah." So it was something worse, something outside her control, which was extra scary since she was powerful and had an answer for everything… except this time.

Worry settled on my shoulders and soaked into my bones. Maybe I could look into what was going on when we were done with my parents' disappearance. I shuddered.

But what if it couldn't wait that long?

# CHAPTER 12

The next morning, I'd barely gotten out of bed—okay, so it was ten o'clock, but there wasn't much reason for me to get up early—when Will walked into the kitchen. "You're up early."

"Yeah, yeah, Mr Sarcasm. You're just jealous."

He grinned. "Busted."

"What are you doing here? Shouldn't you be at work?"

"I was, and I got another call about more burglaries. There's one in particular we've been ordered to investigate. We'll need to check out a few of the others, too, but Imani and another agent are going to help out with the rest of those, make our caseload a bit lighter."

I swallowed the last of my coffee. "What's so special about that specific one?"

"It's for a rich, prominent person in the community. He, his wife, and kids were away on holidays for a month, and they've come back to find their home burgled. The value of what was taken is pretty hefty, so I've been told, and there's no security video. The recordings have been wiped, apparently."

"How do we know it's the same culprit? Maybe this is a normal house-robbing event? I mean, expensive houses would be more of a target anyway. The other burglaries have been less… ambitious." I magicked my cup and bowl clean and into the cupboard.

Will rested his hands on the back of the chair next to me. "Well, it hasn't been confirmed yet, but it's two blocks from one of the streets that were hit a couple of weeks ago. Also, they had a pair of eclectus parrots—male and female. They're gone, yet the front door was shut and locked."

"I have a lot of questions." His information didn't prove anything. What about the person feeding them, because I doubted you could leave enough seed and water for a month? The person feeding the birds might have stolen the stuff, or accidentally let them out and didn't want to say anything.

"I bet you do. If you behave, I might let you ask the victims some of them."

"Promises, promises."

He smirked and gazed at my foxy sleepwear—and, no, it wasn't a euphemism for sexy. I had sky-blue flannelette pyjamas with little orange foxes all over them. "Ready?"

I stood. "Yep. Are you?" I made my doorway.

Will's eyes widened, and he grabbed my arm. "You wouldn't!"

I grinned. "I totally would."

"All right, bluff met. Please get changed into your uniform."

I patted his cheek and smirked. "It's okay to lose. I'm surprised you're not used to it yet." He raised a brow. I snapped my fingers, returning my pyjamas to my bedroom and putting my uniform on.

"Hmm, do I have to keep score now?"

"Suit yourself. Anyway, where was I going to make my doorway to? I have no idea where we're going." I laughed.

"Argh, bested by an amateur. That really does hurt." He straightened his shoulders. "It's okay, though. I'll get you back when you least expect it." His wolfish grin, rather than scaring me, made me want to kiss him. *Ahem.* "Come on, then." He made a doorway, and I stepped through first… to the PIB reception room. I should've known that's where we were going. From there, we made our way to the basement and his Range Rover.

We drove for about ten minutes. He pulled into a typical countryside laneway and slowed, looking intently at the houses on the right side of the street. When we reached number eight, he pulled into the driveway. The metal gates hung from stone-block pillars. An intercom sat to our right on a black steel pole. He pressed the buzzer and introduced himself. The gates swung slowly inward.

The driveway wasn't that long, considering the fanfare of the large gates. A three-storey orangey-brick early twentieth century home sprawled in front of us. Will parked in front of the detached triple garage. I magicked my camera and notebook to myself. Will looked at me as if to say, you're hopeless. "Hey, at least I remembered before we went inside. I'd call that a win." I grinned.

We hopped out. Gravel crunched under my black boots as we walked to the front door. Small and pretty multi-coloured-glass panels above the door created a cottagey feel, even though the home was probably twice the size of Angelica's. The security camera sitting to the right and just above the front door was hard to miss. Shame it'd been tampered with, although even if we'd seen who'd done it, they likely had their face covered. None of my photos so far had shown anything. Would we get lucky today?

Will rang the bell. After a minute, a tall man answered the door. He had at least two inches on Will, and even though his thick dark hair had that salt-and-pepper look, he was still handsome. Not that I was looking, and I didn't go for older men, but I could see that he was attractive. He had on a white T-shirt, blue jeans, and a navy cardigan. Casual clothes, maybe, but they had the look of wealth in the cut and detailing. If his clothes hadn't given it away, his brown leather boat shoes did. The only people I ever saw wearing those were rich people. Not that it mattered. He was allowed to be rich.

"Lily, whenever you're ready?" I looked up at Will. His brow wrinkles deepened, and the man was looking at me like I was an idiot.

"Oh, sorry. Just thinking." I gave a helpless smile, then walked inside.

"Where do you want to start?" the man asked. If I'd

listened earlier, I'd know his name. If I had to get his attention, it was going to be embarrassing.

Will said, "We'll ask you some questions first, *Mr Painter*." Will gave me a quick side-eyed glance, which spoke volumes. If only he didn't know me so well. "When we're done, we'll take some photographs and inspect the property."

"Okay, then. Come through to the library. My wife and children aren't here right now, so we won't be interrupted." Right, to the library. I wasn't jealous. Not. At. All.

The library was a large room with, you guess it, floor-to-ceiling timber shelves filled with books. A maroon rug covered the timber floor, and furniture consisted of two Chesterfields and a black leather armchair with a pouf. Two smoking tables completed the seriously masculine space. Even the ceiling was manscaped, covered in dark timber panels.

He waved at one of the Chesterfields, so Will and I sat there. Mr Painter sat on the other Chesterfield, leaned back, and spread his arm across the back of the chair. He kind of man-spread too. Well, not kind of. He did. Opening his crotch for all the world to see. I was betting he was a space hog on the train.

I placed my camera next to me and got my pen and pad out, ready to take notes. Will sat back and rested his arm on the chair arm. He might have been trying to exude the same relaxedness as Painter. Thankfully, he didn't go the whole way—his legs stayed closed. "When did you first notice something was missing?"

"Last night, when we got back from skiing in Aspen."
Was he trying to make me jealous? I loved the snow, not that
I'd had much chance to go. I'd been on a school excursion
once, when I was fourteen, and I'd been on two long-
weekend trips with my friends from home, but it was around
a six-hour drive from Sydney and pretty damned expensive,
so we didn't make a habit of it. Not to mention our ski
seasons were only three-months long.

"And what time would that have been?"

"Around eight. I was on the phone to our security
company—they were informing me that they'd been around
at six to check things out because our alarm had alerted
them. I didn't turn my phone on until we got home, and
that's when the call came through. At the same time, my
wife was putting some things away in our bedroom when I
heard her scream."

"Was the thief still there?" Good old Will, asking the
question that was pinging around my brain.

Painter shook his head. "No, why?"

"Ah, nothing. Go on." Ha ha, because she was screaming. Who screams when something goes missing? Oh my
God, I can't find my deodorant. *Arghhhhhhhhhh*! I pressed my
lips together so I wouldn't laugh. I was a horrible, horrible
person. Maybe something sentimental had been stolen, like
an urn full of ashes. My mirth evaporated.

"I went up to see what the commotion was, and she was
standing in front of our walk-in closet crying. I asked what
was wrong, and she could hardly speak." Oh, God. I'd
forgotten to go to the toilet at home, and I'd had my coffee.

Would it be rude to interrupt for that? And how embarrassing, asking to use a stranger's toilet. "Her collection of designer handbags was gone. Must be twenty-thousand pounds' worth. And they're all latest season, so they'll fetch a pretty penny on the net."

"You have insurance?" Will asked as I sucked in everything downstairs. Oh, God, why, why had I forgotten to go?

"Yes, we do. But putting in a claim, it's painful." Hmm, I think that would be classed as first-world problems, but anyway....

"Was there anything else taken?"

"Two of my Rolexes. Amanda's sapphire-and-diamond bracelet and matching earrings, a diamond-and-ruby brooch, a silly little felt dragon one of the kids made me for Christmas, and Areola and Pip, our pair of eclectus parrots. I've already fired my security company. They said they couldn't see anything out of the ordinary, that everything looked fine from the outside." Did he just say one of those birds was called *areola*? That was even more shocking than the fact that he just dissed a present from one of his kids.

Will and I looked at each other, and he coughed. I couldn't make any sudden moves because I was busting. I really would have to say something soon. Was there a way you could magic your stuff to the toilet from inside yourself without actually going? My mouth dropped open. That would be brilliant! Hmm, knowing me, I'd remove half my bowel with it and die. Maybe I should just let that idea go. A wave of desperation pushed against my resolve, and I clenched harder.

Will looked at me, furrowing his brow. "Are you all right?"

Oh, God, how could he tell? "Um, yes." My voice wasn't *that* strained. If I told myself that enough, I'd believe it. Gah. I couldn't ask to use the toilet. I'd be embarrassed all day.

"Lily, you're pulling the weirdest face. You look... tortured. And why can't you stop squirming?"

Oh, for God's sake. I looked at Painter. I supposed my embarrassment of asking would be way better than if I ruined his lovely sofa or magically disembowelled myself. "Can I please use your bathroom?" There, it was out, like something else would soon be.

His face said, I'd prefer not, but his mouth said, "Yes, sure. It's just down the hall, second door on the left."

"Thank you. Please excuse me for a moment." I jumped up and clenched my cheeks together as I speed-waddled out of the room. Thankfully he could count, and it was the second door on the left. I did what I had to do, and my relief was stronger than my embarrassment. When I was done, I washed my hands and magicked any odour out of the bathroom. It was bad enough everyone knew I was in the toilet. I did not want to leave anything for them to remember me by. Next time, I would go to the toilet before I left the house. After that I would develop a spell so that I didn't have to go to the toilet. Why hadn't anyone done it yet? Okay, so that meant it was probably near impossible, but I'd never let that stop me before.

As I made my way back down the hall, at a more sedate

pace, a white cat came along and tried to walk between my legs. I stopped and bent to pat it. "Hello, kitty. Aren't you gorgeous." She purred. "I'd love to stand here and pat you all day, but I'm here for work, so I'm going to have to say goodbye."

I continued into the library. Will's expression confirmed he was rather displeased. I gave him a fake smile and sat. "Who were you talking to?"

"The cat."

Painter stared at me. "We don't have a cat."

"Are you sure?" Okay, so that was a stupid question on my part because the man should know whether he had a cat or not, but to be fair to me, I did just see a white cat.

His lip lifted on one corner, confirming that he also thought it was a stupid question. "Of course I'm sure." He turned an irritated gaze on Will. "Is she right in the head?"

Will clamped down on his poker face. I was sure there were so many answers he wanted to give, but he was trying to behave. This interview was going downhill faster than you could say double-chocolate muffin. Mmm, I could really go one of those right now. "She is… usually sane." He turned to me. "Lily, are you sure you saw a cat?"

"Yes. It was white and fluffy. Very friendly, actually. I even patted it."

Painter stood. "Excuse me for a moment." He left the room and came back a couple of minutes later. "I've looked around the place, and there is no white cat. If you've taken drugs before coming to work…."

My mouth fell open. "I have not taken any drugs. I don't

do drugs and never have." I could argue about this white cat till he kicked us out, but it wasn't going to prove anything. "Look, I really did see a white cat, and I'm not on drugs. Maybe a neighbour's cat just snuck into your house or something. I really think we need to focus on the interview."

Will raised a brow. "Oh, you do, do you? How refreshing." He looked up at Painter. "I'm sorry about all this. Why don't we ask you a few more questions, then we can gather our evidence and get out of your hair."

"Are you sure you're capable?"

Will gave Painter a confident stare. "Yes. Look, if my colleague said there was a cat, there was a cat. Whether it was meant to be in here or not is another thing. But that is not a point we're going to continue on. You've had property stolen, and we need to find out who did it. I would appreciate your cooperation." Ooh, he stuck up for me. Would it be unprofessional of me to plant a big, sloppy kiss on his cheek?

Painter pressed his lips together. Finally, he said, "Fine. What else would you like to ask?"

"Do you have photos of any of the items or parrots?"

"Yes. I thought you'd ask." He reached into his pocket and pulled something out. "Here's a memory stick. All the photos are on there. If you need to print it, you can do it at your station." Hey, big spender. Also, he thought we were like the regular police. Oh well, whatever. He really wasn't growing on me. I kind of wished I hadn't left his bathroom in so nice a condition.

Will put it in his inside jacket pocket. "Have you been

threatened by anyone in the last year, or have you made any enemies?"

"I'm a successful businessman, Mr Blakesley. There are always those who are jealous and wish they had what I had, but no, not lately. There was one incident three years ago, but that was settled. He threatened me, so I went to the police. After they cautioned him, I never heard from him again. I would think you should be looking at the fact that my property is an attractive target and go from there." *Wow, thanks for the clue.* I bit the inside of my cheek to keep from commenting. If it were that easy to solve these things, why didn't he know who it was?

"Right. Mr Painter, do you owe anyone money? Maybe they came to collect what was owed?" I managed to keep my mouth closed, but my eyes shot open wider than a Bug-Eyed Sprite. Go, Will! Looked like I wasn't the only one who had trouble keeping the disdain safely inside.

His gaze turned waspish. "How dare you insinuate—"

Will held up his hand in a hang-on-a-minute gesture. His calm tone was a stick poking at a hive. "I have to ask these questions. They're standard in burglaries. We have to find out why you were targeted. It could be random.... It might not be. We're here to do our job, and if that offends you, I'm sorry. Now, can you answer the question, please?"

"No, of course not." He folded his arms. *Not so relaxed now, are we?* It struck me, belatedly, that he was the victim here, but that didn't mean we had to pander to him. He wasn't very nice, and maybe there was a clue in his past dealings. It was just common sense really. Shame he didn't seem to have it.

"Thank you. Right, that's all the questions we have for now. Can you show us where the items were taken from?"

Something touched my calf, and I started. I looked down and grinned. "Hello, kitty who doesn't exist. What are you doing here? Missed my pats?" I knew a sneaky little I-told-you-so smile was on my face, but I didn't care. I looked up at Will—who'd at least stood up for me—and Painter. "So, I guess an apology is in order?" Maybe I shouldn't have said that, but who cared? He'd accused me of being on drugs, for goodness' sake. His default setting was probably always thinking he knew better. News flash, buddy, but you don't.

He stared angrily at the cat, then at me. "I wasn't to know. That's not my cat. I've never seen that cat before." I knew I wasn't the smartest person ever, but I was pretty sure that was not an apology. Whatever.

Will smiled. "I should've known there was a white cat. Sorry for doubting you."

"It's okay. At least you defended my honour." I raised a brow and glared at Painter. I gave the cat one last scratch behind the ear. "Why don't we get the scene investigated, then we should probably take this cat to the local vet, see if it has a microchip. It doesn't have a collar or tag."

"Good idea, Lily." He looked at Wasp Man. "Do you have a laundry we can put the cat in until we leave, so it doesn't wander off again?"

Wasp Man stood. "Yes." Without a second look at me or the cat, he strode out.

I bent down and looked at the white cat. "I guess you're coming with me, then." I picked it up, wary of any signs of impending attack. Thankfully, the cat didn't seem to mind. I cuddled her to my chest and hurried out the door. The house was so big, I could be looking around for the laundry for ages. Painter's footsteps echoed from down the hall, so I followed.

When I reached him, he was standing at an open door, his arms folded. "In here." His manner was abrupt. Why I expected anything else, who knew? Hmm, how right was his assertion that he didn't have any enemies we had to worry about. If the guy treated everyone like he treated Will and me, the enemies list was likely at least a novel long.

I placed the cat inside. "I'll be back soon. Okay?" I stepped back and shut the door, Painter already standing down the hall, tapping his foot, waiting. Will stood further down the hall, observing. He was always looking out for me. Warmth pulsated through my stomach. *How lucky am I!*

"Where to now?" Will asked.

Painter turned to him. "This way." He strode past Will and to the entry foyer where he took the grand staircase to the next level. He showed us his bedroom and the walk-in closet. I took photos, and Will did his thing. The irritating homeowner wouldn't leave. He either had trust issues or control issues. My guess? Probably both. So Will pretended to look intently at things whilst he was actually looking for a magic signature. I photographed everything, and as in many of the other cases, nothing showed up.

"Where were the birds?" I asked. I figured I should photograph that space too.

"In the conservatory."

Will gave me a nod, then turned to Painter. "Can you show us that now? Then I need to see all the doors to outside. Then we'll be done."

Painter didn't so much as grunt. He turned, and out we all went, back down the stairs, and through towards the back of the home. We stopped in a gorgeous glass room with shiny black-and-white marble floors. The white structural frame on three sides of the square room soared overhead, a chandelier dangling from the highest point. The outside wall of the home onto which this was attached was rough stone blocks. The whole effect was dreamy. I officially wanted to take this room home with me. I wondered if he'd miss it.

"They were supposed to be in here." He indicated a humungous white dome-shaped birdcage in one corner. It was big enough for two people. At least his birds had somewhere decent to hang out. His brow furrowed. I tried to push back the sympathy that welled up inside me, but it didn't work. Damn it! He was sad to lose his parrots. That made him a bit more human than he'd been before.

I pointed my camera at the birdcage. *Show me the birds getting out the last time.* Oh, dear. A woman in dark blue slacks, white shirt, and brown cardigan was standing by the cage, her mouth wide open in surprise. Her rounded back spoke of an age over seventy, which meant that her short brown hair must be dyed. She held a small bag of birdseed protectively to her chest as one green and one blue-and-red parrot, wings spread, flew from the cage. I didn't want to give anything away, but I had to ask something to make sure I was looking at the person who was supposed to feed the birds rather than tempt them away. I clicked off a couple of shots and lowered my camera. "Who was feeding your birds while you were away?"

"Why does it matter?"

"We may need to interview them." That probably wouldn't be a bad idea. If that woman in the picture had seen the birds last, we did need to know if she'd seen anything, and where the birds actually had been when she left. We could conduct the interview privately so Wasp Man didn't learn her secret—that she may have been responsible for letting them loose. Let him think a burglar had stolen them.

"My wife's mother, but I'd prefer if you didn't bother her. She's a nervous woman. I don't think she'd like to talk to the police. Besides, I can't see how it matters."

"That's because you're not in law enforcement." Oops, that just slipped out. Will looked at me, his face serious, but there was a definite lip twitch. I didn't want any more pain from Wasp Man, so I straightened my back and put my hands on my hips. A little sass never hurt anyone. "Sounds to me like you're trying to hinder an investigation. Maybe you're happy to claim the insurance? Maybe your wife was sick of her jewellery and wanted some new stuff?" Will's almost-amusement fled in the face of irritation. Had I just gone too far?

Hmm, maybe not.

Wasp Man ran a finger under the collar of his white T-shirt. Had I hit a nerve? Will's crankypants expression turned to curiosity. Painter cleared his throat, and he frowned. "Of course not. I can afford to buy my wife what-ever the hell she wants. I don't need insurance money."

"I see." I nodded. "So, do you have your mother-in-law's phone number?"

"Just a moment." He turned and went back the way we'd come.

Will laughed quietly. "You're full of surprises. Just when I think I'm angry at you, I'm not. How do you do it?"

I batted my eyelashes and smiled innocently. "Magic?"

All frivolity ended when Painter returned. "Here." He shoved a piece of paper at me.

I smiled and took it. "Thank you." I'll admit that I let a little bit of smug slide into my expression. Could anyone blame me?

Will held out his hand. "We're done here. Thank you for your time."

Painter took it and shook. I just gave him a nod. I didn't need to prove I was one of the boys. Shaking hands was overrated. Also, I didn't trust that he'd washed his hands last time he'd used the bathroom. Men—you couldn't trust them with that stuff sometimes. Although, having said that, I'd been in more than one toilet and heard the woman next to me flush and walk out without washing. I liked to think those women had hand sanitiser in their bag, but I knew they couldn't all have. At least we didn't have to shake each other's hands.

I gathered the white cat as we left. It would be terrible if the cat escaped, so I drew on my magic just before walking out the front door. I imagined a force in the shape of a cage around Whitey—so unoriginal, but she must already have a name, and I didn't want to try too hard. I did need to call her something other than "Cat" though. When the *cage* came into being, it made my grasp of Whitey awkward— the force pushed against my will to keep it there. It was as if the energy didn't want to be contained. Thankfully Painter had already shut the door as I fought with the difficult power. Whitey got a fright, too, and fell against the side of the cage, making it tip. Oh crap.

The invisible cage slid out of my arms.

Will jumped in front of me and grabbed the cat, his mouth opening when he felt the vibrating surface. He managed a better hold than I had, and the cat survived the rest of the walk to the car. Will put the cage in the back of the car, and I sat there, too, sweat dampening my forehead from the effort of maintaining the spell.

"What are you doing?"

"Sitting with the cat. She must be scared. Oh, that reminds me." I increased the flow of magic and whispered, "Bring me the cat cage from Angelica's, and put Whitey inside it. Release the invisible cage." It would make her happier and less freaked out if she could see what she was contained by, and the minute tremors of energy would've been off-putting too. Lucky I'd remembered the old plastic cage in her shed. Whitey hissed at the change over but then sat, vigilant but calmer.

"Suit yourself." He shut the door, went around to the driver's side, and got in. He put his belt on and turned to look at me. "What do you think?" He gave a nod at the cage.

"I'm betting this cat belongs to one of our burglary victims. It's just too much of a coincidence."

"You've got an active imagination. It could just be a neighbour's cat. The simplest answer is usually the right one."

I tilted my head to the side and looked into the cage as Will drove up to the gates, which had already opened—someone was eager to get rid of us. I giggled but then calmed myself because I didn't want Whitey to think I was laughing at her, or him. "Are you a boy or a girl? Hmm… not much of a talker, hey?" I looked up into the rear-view mirror, meeting Will's gaze, and was thrown back to the early days of our relationship when we got on each other's nerves… at least that's what we told ourselves back then. "Would be handy to have Mill chat to this one and find out where she's from."

"I'll postpone our other interviews so we can get her back to the PIB. If she really is from next door, we can drop her off later, but if we take her to a vet and she belongs to one of our victims, I don't want to have to explain every-thing. We can find out what we need to know about her… or him—"

"Whitey."

"You've named it?"

"For convenience. Plus it's rude to keep calling it 'it' or 'cat.'"

"It's a cat. It probably doesn't care."

"Well, I do."

He rolled his eyes. "Okay, well, we can find out everything about *Whitey* at headquarters."

On the way back, Whitey meowed a few times, and I chatted to her, hoping that was calming her rather than making her feel worse. Poor kitty. She must've been scared —not only was she with strangers, but she was locked in a cage, and in a conveyance most cats hated... a car.

As soon as we got back, we took her to the sick bay. I'd suggested we take Whitey to Will's office, but he was worried she might do her business there. I didn't see why it mattered —he could clean it up with magic.

I placed the cage on an examination bed. Millicent was out, but Beren was here, and whilst he couldn't talk to animals, he'd be able to tell us if there was a microchip and whether the cat was healthy.

I looked into the cage. "Hey, Whitey. We're going to find out a bit more about you, but don't worry, you're safe." Whitey looked at me from her position jammed at the back of the cage. She was clearly not comforted by my words. I frowned. Poor thing. I straightened and looked at Beren. "Just be careful. She's scared."

"Yeah, thanks for that. I really wouldn't have known if you hadn't told me." Beren stuck his tongue out, then laughed. I rolled my eyes. Okay, so he had a point. "I'll put her to sleep while we do this. She won't feel a thing." His magic vibrated against my scalp, and he whispered something I couldn't quite catch. Whitey blinked a couple of times; then her eyes shut, and she was out. And, yes, I didn't know if it was a boy or girl, but calling the cat "it" was just weird.

Beren opened the cage and gently slid her out. Will put the cage on the floor, leaving a clear space for Beren to work. Gah, I hated hovering uselessly, so instead of worrying in the way, I moved to a chair. Will looked at me. "Why don't you go grab a coffee? Maybe grab me one and B a tea." He never asked me to grab him things, so I knew this was because he could tell I was at a loose end. Waiting patiently, as we all knew, was not my strong point.

I smiled and stood. "That sounds like a great idea. I'll be back in about ten minutes." My plan was to drink the coffee downstairs and get theirs to go. Which was what I did. By the time I returned, Beren was putting Whitey back in the cage. Once the cage was locked, he woke her up.

"Here you are." I handed them their beverages. "What's the verdict?"

Beren walked to a chair and sat. Will magically moved two chairs over to Beren, to form a little circle, and we joined him. Beren had a sip of his tea before he got to it. "We're in luck—she had a microchip. She's also a healthy cat, around four years old, although her teeth are slightly worn. The major thing I'm interested in, though, is that there are two spells on her, one of them is embedded in her brain." Beren smiled. "And, they just happen to bear the same magic signature as our burglar."

My eyes widened. "Oh, wow, B." I didn't know what else to say. This was a major breakthrough. There were many people with missing heirlooms and beloved pets who needed our help. "Do you know what they do?"

"One is a no-notice spell. The other, I'm not entirely sure, but it looks like some kind of communication spell. Whoever stole this cat wanted it to understand what they were saying, and they didn't want anyone to notice it leaving."

"But to what end with the communication spell?" Will asked. "That's the real question."

"Maybe whoever it was just wanted to be the king or queen of their own castle? Maybe no one listens to them and they wanted lots of pets who did?"

Will made an "I don't think so" face. "Why wouldn't they just buy or adopt a few pets and just be nice to them? I'm pretty sure you'd get a similar result."

I shrugged. "They're probably too poor to buy all those pets. And maybe they really, really wanted to converse with them. I mean, it's nice to chat to animals, but it's so much nicer when they chat back. So, are we going to contact the lucky owner and tell them we've found their cat?"

"I think it's more likely that they wanted the pet to leave with them without trouble. Wouldn't it be easier to steal an animal if they left quietly on their own four paws rather than scratching and biting?" Will held up his phone. "I'm just waiting on Liv to get back to me with the phone number. The microchip records had a name and address but no number."

I looked at Beren. "Can you decipher exactly what the spell is?"

"I'd have to research a grimoire. I've magicked a 3D image of it and put it into our database to come back to. I don't have time right now. I might ask Ma'am if she can get one of our specialists onto it. By the time we catch whoever did this and take them to trial, we'll have an answer."

Whitey meowed. "We should take her home."

Beren cleared his throat. "You're right. It's a girl."

I grinned. "I didn't mean to be. It just felt right to say 'she.' I will say that being awesome just comes naturally to me." I waggled my eyebrows. Beren cringed, and Will groaned and rolled his eyes. "Wow, so much angst. No need to be jealous."

Will shook his head. "I just can't. You're impossible." His phone rang. "Hi, Olivia. What've you got for me?" He wrinkled his brow, deep, concerned furrows that made him even more handsome, if that was possible. Who knew worrying could be such a sexy look? Probably all those James Dean fans. Okay, so I was slow sometimes. Will hung up and looked at me. "There was no phone number with the registration, so we're out of luck. Ready to take a drive and visit"—he looked at a message on his phone—"Mrs Allingham?"

"I dare say I am. But before we go, I just need to use the bathroom." Yeah, I wasn't going to make that mistake twice.

ON THE WAY TO VISIT MRS ALLINGHAM, I SAT IN THE BACK with Whitey, who, I was amused to find out, was called Marshmallow Kitty Allingham. She had a middle name. I felt slighted by this—my parents hadn't seen fit to give me one, yet this cat had one. She was obviously a cherished member of her family.

After just over thirty minutes, Will pulled into a driveway off a main thoroughfare through Chaldon, which was still only a single lane each way. The only time you got wide roads around here was when you were on the motorway. A throwback to a time when horse and cart were the done thing.

There was no gate, but the driveway ambled for twenty metres, crowded on both sides by unkempt shrubs and huge trees. Garden beds, which were little more than strips of dirt, lined the walls under her front windows. Paint peeled off the timber windows, and rusted holes marred the gutter. Such a tired little brick bungalow. Sadness deflated my joy at bringing her home. "Gee, Marshmallow, I hope your owner is okay." I looked at Will in the rear-view mirror. "This doesn't look like a very safe place to have a pet, let alone a human."

My sorrow was mirrored in his grey eyes. He blew out a breath. "I know. But maybe it's better on the inside than it looks out the outside?" I didn't say anything. We both knew that probably wasn't the case.

Will got out of the car and shut his door. I stared at

Marshmallow, snug but sitting as far back in her cage as she could. "I don't want to leave you here, but if your mum wants you, I'm going to have to. But you're in good condition, so I bet she takes very good care of you and you miss her. Come on, then." I opened my door, grabbed the cage, and slid out of the car.

As we reached the front door, Marshmallow yowled. It was an unhappy sound. "Do you think she's desperate to see her family?"

The worry divots between his eyes activated. "I can't speak cat. If only Mill was here. But that doesn't sound like a happy cat noise to me."

Will was about to knock on the door. I knew it wouldn't be right to get back in the car and steal this lady's cat a second time, but I didn't want to leave her here. "Are you sure this is the right address? Maybe Mrs Allingham moved? Maybe we should just get back in the car and go home?"

He folded his arms and stared me down, as if I were a child about to get a talking to. His voice started loudly to be heard over Marshmallow's yowling. "No, no, and third time, no, Lily. We are not keeping the cat. She belongs here." His voice had become decidedly softer by the end of his rant. This place and Marshmallow's reaction were getting to him too. "Sorry." He looked at the cat as he said that.

Then, he knocked on the door.

Damn.

We didn't have to wait long before a grey-haired woman answered it. She was a bit shorter than me and wore a long brown wool skirt and a black polo-neck jumper. She wasn't fat, just solid. What hit me when she opened the door was the stench of animal urine and wet-dog smell. I tried not to gag because it wouldn't be polite. It was all I could do to not run with the cage back to the car. Piles of newspapers lined the hallway on one side behind her. Oh dear, she was a hoarder, unless old newspaper piles were a new decorating fad I hadn't heard about.

She smiled. "Hello. What can I do for you?"

I struggled to hold onto the cage as Marshmallow fell back, maybe trying to get out of the rear of the cage. She could probably smell the other cats that were no doubt using the house as their litter box.

"I'm Agent Blakesley from the PIB." She must've been a witch if he was introducing himself like that. I used my second sight. Yep, she was. Why couldn't she clean her house then? "I'm looking for a Mrs Allingham. Does she live here?"

The woman pressed her lips together, thinking. "Hmm, not unless she's invisible." She laughed. "I've lived here for thirty years, and my name isn't Allingham."

"Oh, what is it, then?" Will asked.

"Pryor. Daphne Pryor. Pleased to meet you, Agent Blakesley." She held her hand out for him to shake. Ew, where had that hand been? If it was anywhere inside that house, Will would have to disinfect himself afterwards.

He slowly put his hand out and was quick to retract it once the obligatory deed was done. "Do you know of any Mrs Allinghams around here?"

"Mmm, might've been one living up the road a few

years ago, but I can't be certain. I'm sure there's a way you government people can find out though." She bent and peered at the cage. "What've you got there?"

I lifted the cage and held it to my chest, protectively. "Um, Mrs Allingham's cat. That's why we're looking for her." I shrugged and made my voice as nonchalant as possible. "I'm sure we'll find her. If not, I have a friend who's looking for a cat, and she loves white." Okay, so I was laying it on a bit thickly, but it appeared as if this woman owned several animals, and I didn't want her asking if she could have this one. Not that Will would give Marshmallow to her. We still had to find Mrs Allingham. But what if she'd died, someone else took the cat, and no one had updated the records? Crap.

"We won't take any more of your valuable time, Ms Pryor. We have to find Mrs Allingham, so we'll be off. Have a good afternoon." Without waiting for her answer, he turned and started for the car. I was right next to him the whole way.

She called out "Bye" as we reached the car, and a faint dog bark came from inside. I shuddered. I would not be comfortable until we were locked in the car and driving away. To think any poor animals were in that house. Why couldn't the burglar be out here saving some animals? As soon as we were safe in the Range Rover, I buckled in. "Should we report her to someone? Is there a special animal cruelty organisation we can call?"

"Yes. We'll do it tomorrow morning. This afternoon, we have a lot more digging to do."

"To find Mrs Allingham?"

He drove out of the driveway and turned onto the street. "Yes."

I relaxed back into the seat. Good riddance to that place. "You're a clever cat, Marshmallow." She'd stopped yowling. Now she was only cowering in the back of the cage. "You don't like the car either. I'm sorry we're putting you through this. It's looking like you'll have to suffer a few more car trips before we find your owner."

"Maybe she died and left the cat to someone else, or maybe her address was recorded incorrectly when they did the microchipping?"

"That's what I was thinking, about the dying bit. I guess that's easy enough to check."

"Yes, it is. Can you call Olivia and get her to run a check?"

"Yes, boss."

"You're finally admitting it, then."

"What?"

"You're acknowledging that I'm the boss." He smirked.

"Yep. That's what I want you to think." I smiled sweetly. "You catch more flies with honey, so they say. Now, if you don't mind, I have a call to make." I poked my tongue out. He shook his head but smiled.

I called Liv and asked her to search for a living or a dead Mrs Allingham, who may or may not have ever lived near or at Ms Pryor's house. After I hung up, Will's phone rang. He answered via the Range Rover's Bluetooth. "Hello, Agent Blakesley speaking."

A female voice came through... a rather breathy voice that I recognised. "Oh, Agent Blakesley, I'm so glad you answered. It's Fee here. I'm sure you remember me."

Will's gaze flicked to mine in the rear-view mirror, and he cleared his throat. "Ah, yes. What can I do for you?" He cringed. Oops. He'd just given her an open invitation to ask whatever she wanted. I didn't know whether to laugh or be annoyed. I supposed I should get used to women hitting on him. Who could blame them? At the end of the day, he loved me, and I could trust him.

"I was wondering if I could drop a lemon drizzle cake to you at your work? I appreciate the job you're doing trying to find my boy. Also, have you found anything yet?"

"Ah, thanks for the thought, but I'm out this afternoon, and all day tomorrow, and probably the day after that too. We're following some leads, but there's not much more I can say. We'll be sure to let you know as soon as we find something."

"Oh." Her voice sounded deflated. "Okay, then. But you will call if you find anything?"

"Of course. Straight away."

"Thank you. He means the world to me. Goodbye."

She hung up before Will could say anything. Gah, now I felt sorry for her. She was just lonely and missing her beloved companion. Marshmallow gave a soft meow. I peered into the cage. Another animal we had to reunite with their owner. We really need to find Mrs Allingham. "Don't worry, Marshmallow. We'll figure this out soon, and then you can go home."

We were about to pull into headquarters when Liv called back. "Hey. Any news on Mrs Allingham?" I asked.

"I'm afraid not, Lily. The only address I could find was the one you already have, and there are no death records for her. Maybe she's in a nursing home or something? She's fifty-eight, which is kind of young for that, but you never know."

"Ah, okay. She could even be on holidays, but I know she doesn't live at that address."

"She could've moved and not updated her voting records. It happens."

I sighed. "Okay. Thanks for checking it out. We're just here now. I'll come up and see you in five."

"Okay. See you soon."

Will showed his ID to the guy at the gate, then drove through. "No luck, huh?"

"Nope. So now what?"

"Well, we get Marshmallow into headquarters, grab a coffee, then get to our next lot of interviews."

Horror at the cat's plight rumbled through me. "You're not going to leave her there overnight in this cage, are you?"

"No! What kind of heartless pig do you think I am?"

"Oh… good. Well, I didn't know. What are you going to do with her, then?"

The roller door for the basement parking opened, and we drove in. "We'll see if we can get someone to take her home for the night. Chances are, we'll track down her owner tomorrow. I might get you onto it. You can work from Millicent's office."

"Okay." I could handle that. It would be nice to have a project that was all mine. I smiled.

Will parked the car, and we got out and into the lift. I took it to the cafeteria floor, and Will went up to his office, carrying Marshmallow's cage. I grabbed a coffee for me, and two teas, just in case Millicent was in. I knocked on her office door with my head and then opened it with magic. Carrying three hot drinks made for difficult multitasking. I supposed I could've magicked the drinks to hover along with me, but that sounded complicated, and I was bound to stuff it up. If you'd ever seen me attempt to juggle, you'd understand.

"Hello!" I called out as I wandered through to the inner office.

"Hello, love." Imani smiled up at me from her spot seated in front of Millicent's desk. She was sitting back in the chair, legs crossed. Millicent sat behind her desk, laptop and paperwork spread out in front of her. Liv was at her desk at the computer. Mill and Liv both smiled and said hello.

I looked at Imani. "Sorry. I didn't know you'd be here. I only grabbed two teas. Would you like my coffee?" I handed the teas to their intended recipients, then held my coffee out to Imani.

She smiled. "No thanks, love. Just had one, actually."

Guilt was an irritating emotion. "You sure?" She nodded. *Okay, Guilt, you heard her. Go away.* "How are your cat-burglar interviews going?" I sat in the spare chair at Liv's desk.

"We had seven in the same street this morning, and we're done. Depending on what comes through later, maybe I can help you with your run. I hear you're behind."

"Yep. A missing cat turned up at one of our interviews this morning. It just happened to have the same magic signature in its brain that we've been finding at the crime scenes. We traced it to a Mrs Allingham, but when we went to her last known address, she didn't live there. Will's going to find someone to take the cat home tonight, and tomorrow, I'll do some more research, try and see if we can find Mrs Allingham."

Liv tilted her head to the side. "Sorry I couldn't find anything useful. I looked on every database I could think of."

"I know. If you found nothing, I probably won't either, but you never know. And you've got a lot of other work to worry about. I don't mind having the extra task. In case you hadn't noticed, work isn't exactly taking off for me now that I had to take my website down." I frowned. Will, Angelica, and I had agreed that it would be safer for me if I just shelved the photographic work for the time being, especially since RP could attack me via the tattoo. Even though we'd fixed that problem, it was clear they were watching me and would follow if I ever left home any normal way. Once—I refused to say *if*—we took care of RP, I'd go back to it. I just had to be patient. The story of my life. "Mill, do you think you could get anything useful if you spoke to Marshmallow?"

"Who's Marshmallow?"

"The cat."

She pressed her lips together, thinking. "What kind of information do you need?"

"An address of where Mrs Allingham lives would be good, or even whether she's still alive. How long the cat's been wandering around, homeless. That kind of thing."

"Time doesn't mean much to animals if they haven't linked to a witch, which would give them our understanding, so that's out. An address would be the same issue. We could ask if she's alive or dead, I suppose. When do you need this done?"

"Now would be good. Only if it's no problem."

She scrunched her nose and looked at all the papers on her desk. "This isn't urgent to solving your case—rehoming animals isn't really a priority, I'm afraid. And I'm kind of in the middle of things right now. If I have time later, I'll let you know. Is that okay?"

I shrugged. "I guess it has to be—it's not urgent, but it's our best lead yet, which is depressing because it's not that great a one. I'm going to look into it more tomorrow anyway. Maybe if you don't get to it today, I'll let you know tomorrow if I can't find anything else."

"Okay. Sounds good. If you can't find anything by tomorrow lunchtime, I'll have a chat to Marshmallow." She smiled.

"Thanks." I turned to Imani. "So, what do you think?"

"About what?"

"The thief. Don't you guys do some kind of profile on

criminals?" I looked at Millicent. "You guys do, do that, don't you?"

Millicent nodded. "Yes, we do, but we haven't in this case because the stakes aren't high enough. If we profiled every criminal case, we'd need to hire ten new agents." Millicent stopped and made a bubble of silence. "We definitely don't have the budget if what Ma'am says is true."

Imani leaned forward. "What did she say?"

Millicent stared at Imani, probably deciding whether to spill or not. *Come on. Come on.* She gave in. Yes! Not much of a secret agent, thank goodness for me. I hated not knowing stuff. "Chad was brought in to cut the budget, which he's done, but apparently it hasn't worked. He's found a way to stuff it up."

"I thought he was brought in to upset Ma'am?" It seemed pretty clear to me. But maybe my point of view was skewed.

Millicent grimaced. "That too, but Angelica has never compromised on things. If she needed agents to do overtime, she pulled them in. Solving crimes and ensuring the safety of her agents is always her top priority."

"Why does money always get in the way?" I hated how the world worked sometimes.

Imani shook her head. "Greed? Maybe the directors get a bonus if they keep operations to a certain budget?"

I narrowed my eyes. "Or someone just wants to hamstring Angelica. Or maybe they want the whole organisation to be less effective?"

Millicent sucked in a breath. "You're not the first one to

think those things, Lily, but for the love of all that's holy, please keep them to yourself. We shouldn't even be talking about this here. What was I thinking?" She shook her head. "Conversation is over. This is what it is. We work with the budget we have, and we don't worry about what the higher-ups are doing. It's none of our business. Understood?"

"Yes, Millicent." I might not be able to talk about it, but I could sure think about it. Why did I have to solve every problem I came across? Maybe it was in my blood. "Okay, then, change of subject. How are my two favourite rats?"

Liv pulled a face, as if to say that no rats could ever be anyone's favourite anything. I grinned. Millicent smiled. "They're doing really well, thank you. Bagel keeps asking about you. She wants to come visit."

I laughed. "She's adorable. I should find time to come say hello. I'd invite her to Angelica's, but I'm not sure how she'd feel about having a rat in her house."

"She won't care. It takes more than a rodent to bother her. She's so contrary, she'd probably pretend to like Bagel just to surprise everyone."

I laughed. "Yep. That definitely sounds like Angelica."

Imani's phone dinged. She slid it out of her pocket and read the message. She looked at me. "We're being called out again this afternoon. Beren and I will be taking some of those cases off your back. Twelve new ones just came in. Another street was hit last night, but the police have only just linked it with the other crimes. We're off to Godstone."

I pulled out my phone and got it up on the map—I still had no idea where everything was around here. "Oh, that's a fair way from here, but it's near Caterham, where that dead pet was found." Damn, thinking about it still made me sad. I hated whoever was doing this. Cruel witch.

There was a knock on the outer-office door, and Beren called out, "Is it safe to come in?"

Millicent laughed. "Why wouldn't it be?"

Beren walked in, smiling. "Well, secret women's business. You know. Liv could be telling you how gorgeous I am, or how good I am in b—"

"Beren!" Liv touched one hand to her darkening cheek. I snickered. She was so cute when she was embarrassed. "I never talk about that stuff." Her eyes were wide in horror.

He laughed. "I know you don't. Just teasing." He bent and gave her a quick kiss on the lips. He didn't usually show affection to her at work—professionalism and all that—but he was probably trying to make up for upsetting her. He had nothing to worry about though—she was crazy about him.

Imani stood. "I guess we'd better get to it, then."

"If you get any good clues, let Will know, would you?" I was desperate to get to the bottom of this one before any more animals were hurt.

"Will do, love. See you later."

Beren waved, and they both left via the normal door. Millicent looked at me. "Don't mind me; I've got work to do."

"Not a problem. Is there anything I can do to help?"

"Not for me, and I think Liv is right too."

Liv gave me a sad smile. "Yep. I'm all good. Sorry."

I shrugged. "It's fine. Will and I are supposed to go back

out into the field anyway—I just don't know when. I'll go find him, and if he's not ready, I might chill at home. I'll see you ladies later." I gave Liv a quick hug and Millicent a wave, then wandered out into the hall and over to Will's office. Luckily, he was in.

"Hey, gorgeous. What are you doing here?" He was sitting behind his desk, his laptop in front of him.

"I see the cat cage is gone."

"Yep. Angela from accounting agreed to take her. Her cat died recently, so she knows how to look after a cat, plus there won't be any issues with other animals in the house… because there aren't any."

"Cool. Um, are we going back out soon?"

"Give me five minutes." He made a couple of phone calls while I waited. Finally, he shut his laptop and stood. The door to his outer-reception room opened. Will stared at the door, and I jerked my head around.

Oh, *great*.

Chad strode into the office and stopped just inside the doorway. He folded his arms and planted a stern gaze on Will. "Why is it taking so long?"

Will blinked. "Excuse me?"

"The investigation into the cat burglaries, and it's *Sir*."

I turned back towards Will and rolled my eyes. This guy was just too much. Way, way too much. Will assumed a poker face Ma'am would have been proud of. "Ah, yes, *Sir*. A few days is hardly a long time for an investigation. We're closing in on the thief, but we're not there yet. May I ask what the sudden rush is?"

"I've had a call from Superintendent Collins. Apparently Painter is a family friend, and he wasn't impressed by your visit, particularly your assistant. I don't need to explain anything more, do I?" I turned at the last and received an angry glare for my troubles. Argh. "So, get out there right now and solve this damned thing before I recommend you be stood down. Get back to me by 11:00 a.m. tomorrow, and you'd better have a result." He jerked his chin up, then spun around, and left.

I made a bubble of silence. "Drama queen."

Will frowned. "Yes, but he calls the shots, so we'd better figure this thing out."

"But he can't fire you because you couldn't find the criminal by the date he ordered. That's insane. Angelica will stick up f—"

He shook his head. "No, she won't. She can't. She's in more trouble than I am right now. Someone wants her gone too—you know that."

I clenched my fists, squeezing all my anger into them. "Why is the world so unfair? Grrrr."

His gaze softened. "And that, my gorgeous lady, is why we won't ever give up. Sometimes we're the difference between justice and no justice. Think of all the criminals who would still be causing havoc if we hadn't been there to stop them?"

I sighed. "You're right." I stood. "Let's not dilly-dally, then. We've got a criminal to find."

AFTER TWELVE MORE INTERVIEWS, I CLIMBED INTO THE Range Rover, sagged against the seat, and yawned. Will shut his door and clicked in his seat belt. He slapped both hands on the steering wheel, and I jumped. "Oh my God! Do you have to do that? You know I could die."

He turned to me, a "what the hell are you talking about?" look on his face. "Now who's the drama queen?"

"I'm hypersensitive to unexpected noises. You know I am. It's like you've just shocked me with a defibrillator, and I don't appreciate it." I rested a protective hand on my chest.

"Look, if you ever die in front of me, I'll bring you back. Okay?"

"Wouldn't it be easier if you didn't kill me in the first place?"

He shrugged. "Maybe, maybe not. Speaking of which, one dead Rottweiler killed defending its home, more stolen goods, yet no new clues, and I'm ready to punch something." His eyes widened. "Not you, of course."

I laughed. "I know. I've never been scared of you, Will. You have to be one of the nicest people I've ever met… once you get past the crankypants demeanour, that is. Anyway, you're not the only one who wants to punch something… or someone. If stupid Chad were here now…."

He made a tut-tut noise. "That wouldn't help anything. He deserves a dressing down, but violence? Unless it's necessary, you'll regret it later. The temporary joy is always followed by crushing guilt, which lasts way longer."

I sighed. "Yeah, yeah, I know you're right. Maybe we could have a boxing session later?"

He smiled. "That's a great idea. I've got some equipment in storage. I'll magic it over to James's home gym. He won't mind if we have a workout." Since Will had decided to stay at Angelica's, he was renting his place out. He'd offered for me to move in with him, but I didn't want to leave Angelica by herself, even though she'd insisted she was fine. She hadn't gone so far as to say she wanted me to leave, and she was the sort of person who would have if that's what she preferred. Besides, she was hardly home anyway, so it wasn't like we didn't get enough privacy. With everything going on at work for her, I was doubly happy I'd decided to stay. That little niggling in my gut told me things were going to get worse before they got better. And then there was everything we had ahead of us with RP....

It was as if a weight pressed on my chest. My breathing sped up. I shook my head to clear the oppressive thoughts and banish the walls that were closing in. "Gah. There's just too much going on. I definitely need to sweat it out and focus on something else." I looked at him. "What if we can't figure this out?"

He grabbed my hand. "Don't worry. He won't fire me. I can talk my way out of it, and if worst comes to worst, I can take on some private security work. Whenever this thing with Angelica gets sorted out, things will get back to how they should be. Don't worry. Our main focus is to solve this case and find the missing items and pets. Don't get sidetracked by anything else... especially idiots." He smiled.

I took a deep breath and smiled back. "Okay. You're right."

His smile widened into a cocky grin. "Always."

My mouth dropped open. "I wouldn't go that far."

His phone rang. "Hello, Agent Blakesley speaking." His forehead crinkled. Not a good sign. He stared straight ahead, out the windscreen. "Are you sure?" Will ran a hand through his hair and put the phone on speaker.

Liv's voice filled the cabin. "Positive. And Sir said you're to get onto it this afternoon. He told me to remind you about what he said earlier."

Will gave me an exasperated look. "Yep, okay. We're onto it. Thanks, Liv. Bye."

The stress rolling off him set my heart beating faster. Things were about to get messy. I just knew it.

# CHAPTER 13

After speaking to Liv, Will drove straight back to headquarters. From there, we magicked ourselves to a toilet in a train station at York, far north of England. From there, we hopped into an Uber to travel the last few miles to where we were headed.

Mrs Allingham's estranged son's place.

The plot thickened.

Will's unhappiness when talking to Liv was because Mrs Allingham's son, Trevor, had been abused by his mother. He'd been put in foster care at thirteen, and as soon as he was old enough, he'd moved far enough away from where he'd lived with his mother that he felt safer. He was now twenty-five.

The Uber turned into a quiet street filled with row upon row of terrace houses in groups of two or three. I couldn't tell if they'd been built in the 1950s or '70s, but every garden was neat enough—many had trimmed hedges as the front fence—and each home looked cared for. Two kids kicking a soccer ball-or *football* as Will always corrected me —on the street ran to the gutter to get out of our way. The driver pulled over a few houses down from them, at number thirty-five, and Will and I got out.

I made sure my return to sender was up—who knew what kind of reception he'd give us, knowing we were looking for his mother? Oh, and had I mentioned he was a witch, and so was his mother?

Will knocked on the front door. He had to knock again before a short, slim man, whose fair hair was already thinning, answered the door. His black T-shirt had ACDC on the front, and his dark blue jeans were clean. His expression was a cross between "I don't care" and wary. "Can I help you?"

Will didn't smile, but he relaxed his poker face to something a bit kinder, less agenty. He held his hand out to shake. "I'm Agent Blakesley from the PIB. I called earlier. This is my assistant, Ms Bianchi." I smiled because one stern agent was enough for anyone. "Do you mind if we come in and ask a few questions about Mrs Allingham?"

Trevor's smile was all sarcasm. And who could blame him? We'd probably already dredged up memories he'd rather not think about… all for a cat? What the hell were we doing? Oh, that's right, Chad and his inability to be fair and reasonable. "Not at all. Come on in." He stood aside to let us enter.

The blinds were shut, making the rooms dark. Dim

bulbs gave us enough light to see by, but it was like being in a bad dream where you couldn't see properly, as if fog hovered, hiding the true nature of where we were. Trevor stopped in the living room. He sat in a worn leather armchair and indicated we should sit on a two-seater lounge, the fabric worn. We sat, and I took in the room as I slid my notepad and pen out of my pocket.

A small flat-screen TV sat in one corner, and a low table next to it, a row of small glass birds lined up neatly on top. Despite everything feeling *faded*, it was clean. The scent of orange blossom wafted in the air, and it looked as if he'd vacuumed recently. Trevor sat forward on his seat, his elbows on his thighs as his fingers picked at the nails of his other hand. He looked at the ground before slowly looking up to meet Will's eyes. "So, what's all this about, then?"

"We're in the middle of an investigation, and we came across Mrs Allingham's cat." That was nice of him to avoid saying "your mother's." Hopefully, Trevor appreciated it and told us whatever he could. "We went to her last known address, but she wasn't there. I understand you're estranged, but do you know where she's living?"

Fear raced across his eyes, then anger and uncertainty. I wanted to tell him we were sorry, but how sorry were we? We were still here asking him these questions despite his obvious pain. "The last time I saw her was when they took me away. We were living in that godawful hovel." He shook his head slowly and stared past Will, a faraway look in his eyes. His eyes glazed over with tears. Then he blinked them away and looked at Will again. "You know, the one thing I wanted was to take those animals with me. The poor bastards."

"What do you mean?" asked Will. My hackles rose. She was cruel to animals, and we were trying to send that poor cat back to her? No. Freaking. Way.

"She collected strays and things—dogs, cats, a budgerigar. She never cleaned up after them, starved them half the time. I wasn't the only one she abused. Whenever I tried to help the pets, she'd beat me. And the conditions we lived in...." He shuddered. "Filthy, piled to the ceiling with rubbish, crap other people didn't want. She loved that stuff more than she did me. When she took up with Bill, it got worse. They'd both shoplift, and he started beating me too."

I sucked in a breath. Will jerked around to stare at me. He blinked, and I was pretty sure we were both thinking the same thing. He turned back to Trevor. "Do you have a picture of your mother?"

He shook his head. "No. She never took any photos, not that I'd want one anyway. It's taken me all this time not to see her evil face whenever I shut my eyes." He looked up at the ceiling. "I'll be back at the counsellor after this." My heart broke for him, and every other child like him. Some people should never have kids.

"I'm sorry to have to ask this, but can you describe her for me? It's important." Will leaned forward slightly, and I was ready to jump out of my seat. He was going to confirm what we already knew—my stomach hummed with it.

Trevor regarded me. "'Bout your height, maybe a bit

shorter, brown hair, parted in the middle. She liked to wear plaits, like a schoolgirl." He sneered and shook his head.

"Does she lie about things?" I was pretty sure Will didn't need to ask that question, but maybe it was all part of gathering evidence you could use in court, a reason we could go back there and investigate further without being accused of harassing her.

"All the time. Once one of my teachers called the police because I'd had a black eye. When they came to see us, she lied about who she was and used her magic to persuade them to leave." He picked at his nails again. "She was always saying how she hated normal people, and who were they to tell her how to bring up her kid. She always thought non-witches looked down on us. I tried to tell her that they had no idea, that if anyone looked down on us, it was because we were poor, but she never listened. She knew best...."

"Right. I really appreciate you being so candid with us, Trevor." Will gave him a gentle smile. "You're a brave lad. I'm sorry life's been less than kind."

He shrugged and looked at the ground. "It's okay now. I have good friends, and I like my counsellor." He looked up again. "The last home I went to was a real nice couple—non-witches, but good people. I go there and visit all the time. Kind of makes up for things." He made a "what can you do?" face.

Will stood, so Trevor and I followed. Will held out his hand and gave Trevor a card. "If you ever need anything, let me know."

Trevor hesitated before taking the card. He smiled. "Thanks. I'm sure I'll be fine, but I appreciate the thought. I hope I helped with whatever it is you're doing."

"You've helped us solve something we wouldn't have been able to otherwise, so, yes, you've helped enormously."

We said goodbye and waited out the front for another Uber. I made a bubble of silence. "So, looks like we've found Mrs Allingham."

Will nodded slowly. "Yep, but there's no way I'm giving that cat back."

"Good, because I would've had to fight you on it." The Uber pulled up, and we got in. My foot tapped the whole way back to the train station—I desperately wanted to continue the conversation. We were on the edge of answers, and I didn't want to forget all the questions I had, which was likely because my brain was like a colander.

At the station, we jumped out of the car and jogged to the toilets—he was as eager as me to figure this out. Within two minutes, we were on one side of the PIB reception-room door while Gus was on the other, opening it for us. "Agent Blakesley, Miss Lily! Lovely to see you." Gus grinned.

"Hey, Gus. Great to see you too. You're working late."

"Yeah. We're understaffed, and they offered me some overtime. The missus wants a new kitchen."

Will smiled, his dimples coming to the fore and sending fuzzy warmth through my stomach. "You know what they say, Gus…. Happy wife, happy life."

"Aye, that they do. Not sure I agree with them, but I do my best." He winked. "Well, have a lovely evening."

"You too. I'll see you later." I waved as Will led the way to the lift.

We went up to his office. Once we were safely there, he called James. My brother, the workaholic that he was, was still on site. I checked my phone—six forty-five. He should be home helping Millicent with the baby and dinner, although, maybe not. When would I stop forgetting that witches could do things just by thinking about it, or, if you wanted to be flamboyant, adding in the click of a finger and thumb? Hmm, thought for the day: lucky we weren't made of the same stuff as match heads—we'd be in real trouble.

Will and I sat on either side of his desk, and he made a bubble of silence. He rested his forearms on the table and folded his hands together. "So, I'm eager to hear what you think."

"I thought you'd never ask. I'm thinking something is off with Daphne Pryor, and not just with her cleanliness. With that description, she's obviously Mrs Allingham. But why lie?"

The outer-office door opened, and James strolled through. Will redid the bubble of silence to include him. James smiled and sat next to me. "What've I missed? How's it all going?"

"Pretty well. We just got a major clue, or maybe just another issue that needs solving." Then I repeated what I'd just told Will.

"So when you guys went there with the cat, she lied?"

"That's about it," said Will. "It would be good to get you to come with us next time." My brother's talent was telling when someone was lying—hence why I got caught out on several occasions when he was still looking after me, and even when we were younger and our parents were around. Even though his magic hadn't come in, he always somehow knew when I wasn't telling the truth. "At this point, we need to work out why she lied, which might be easier if we question her with you present."

"Yeah, but you know we can't force her to even speak to us unless we have a good reason. Tell me what your reasons are." My brother relaxed back into his chair and rested his linked hands on his stomach.

I let Will have the floor, since he was the agent—*big of me, I know*. "Let's see…. Her pet was found miles from her home in another house that's recently been burgled. When we try and return the pet, she denies being the owner. That at least gives us a link."

James folded his arms. "Maybe she dumped the pet and is embarrassed?"

I shook my head. "More like she didn't want to get in trouble for neglect or dumping a cat. She's been in trouble with the police before. Shouldn't Liv have found all that when she looked her up?"

Will wrinkled his forehead. "Her son said she used her magic to persuade people. Maybe she risked it so that the police wouldn't record their dealings? That would take far less persuasion than forcing them to walk away and leave her son in her care, therefore ignoring the situation altogether. If she ever got caught doing that, we'd have thrown her in jail."

"So she did just enough that it wouldn't cause future issues?" Wow, what a piece of work.

"That makes sense." At least James agreed with Will. "Do we have a coincidence or a link?" James looked at me. "Your photos didn't pick much up, did they?"

"Nope." Which was a total bummer. "Is there any way we can question Mrs Allingham at her place? If she is linked to all this, maybe we'll see something that fits—like an animal or item from one of the crime scenes?"

James bit his upper lip. "Possibly, but we can't force her to let us in, and we don't have enough for a warrant. There are too many possible reasons she's lying. Maybe whoever committed those other crimes stole her cat? It seems to be the hallmark of this thief."

My shoulders sagged. James had a good point. "And it's not like she was living in luxury, care of the proceeds of crime. I wouldn't let an animal live in that house." I coughed, the memory of the odour enough to put me off.

Will jerked upright, his eyes bright. "I've got it! We can question her about when her cat went missing. That's a legitimate link to this case. Maybe she's not who we're after, but she could give us some clues maybe? Who knows, it could be one of her friends who's done this. In any case, it would give us an excuse to go back and hopefully find something, even if it's another lead not related to her."

"That's good enough for me." James smiled. "Let's go."

"Do you usually question people at this hour?"

Will's smile was grim. "We do when my job is on the line. Eleven tomorrow morning. Remember?"

I groaned. "Gah, I'd forgotten." I stood. "I just need a toilet stop. Then I'm good to go."

Will laughed. "Yeah, I don't think you'd fancy using Mrs Allingham's toilet."

I shuddered. "Yeah, nah."

I hurried to the bathroom and then met the guys at Will's car. My mouth dropped open, and I planted my hands on my hips in faux outrage. "You're in my seat!" As kids, James and I would always fight about who got to sit in the front seat.

"Ner, ner. First in best dressed." James poked his tongue out, and the window slid up and closed, cutting off any reply I might have had.

I narrowed my eyes and climbed into the back seat, directly behind James. I buckled in.

"What, not going to say anything?" James turned to try and look at me, but he had to twist too far and gave up.

"Nope. You won, fair and square."

"You're lying."

"Maybe…." I giggled. That should scare him sufficiently. He knew I was plotting, and he'd have to be aware for the whole trip. I'd leave my revenge till close to the end, and he knew it. It's what I did when we were kids. Torment me, and I'd find a way to make yours worse. I grinned.

As Will drove, I punched the back of the seat every now and then, making James jump twice. Will smirked both times. "Hey, mate," said James the second time. "Next time she annoys you, there will be zero sympathy from me."

"I'm thinking it will be worth it. This is highly entertaining. It's nice to see someone else suffer for a change." Will laughed.

I shrugged. "He asked for it. He'll think twice before taking my seat next time." *Punch.* Being childish was so much fun.

After a while, I recognised the road—it wasn't far to Mrs Allingham's, so I upped my game. I carefully touched my finger through the gap between the headrest and the seat, tickling the back of his neck. He jerked forward, and I sat back innocently. He rubbed the back of his neck. At this stage, he probably thought it was a random itch or bug. I grinned. I waited a minute, then did it again. He slapped his hand on the back of his neck, then stopped. "Lily!"

I laughed. "Yes? What's wrong?"

Will slowed and put his blinker on. "We're here. Time for you two to act like adults."

"Yes, *Lily.*" James had his big-brother voice activated. I knew he enjoyed the silliness as much as I did—it was a reminder of happier times. We'd both copped plenty of yelling from Mum or Dad at the time, but it was always worth it.

Will parked, and we got out into the frigid night air. I folded my arms, but it didn't help much. I drew on my power, and, voila, my coat appeared. I snuggled into its depths, relishing the amazingness of magic.

More than one dog barked from the dark interior of the house. I looked up, gauging our chances of a bit of natural light, but the clouds obscured the stars and moon. Will used his phone as a torch. I put up my return to sender and followed Will and James to the front door. Will knocked. The dogs barked louder, and one howled.

Will knocked again. Nothing.

"I'll go around the back." James pulled out his gun and went to one side of the house. He scaled the brick fence and disappeared over the other side. The skin on my nape rose into goosebumps, and I shivered. Why did dark houses seem so sinister? It was the same pile of materials forming a building that was there during the day, and back then, it hadn't worried me, except for the stink coming from inside.

Maybe the barking and howling hounds were giving me the creeps?

"Where do you think she is?" I asked Will loudly over the noisy canines. I was pretty sure he didn't know the answer, but nervousness made me want to fill the void with action, even if it was only talking.

"Out robbing more houses?"

Well, that was unexpected. "Do you really think so?"

"Anything's possible, although seeing where she lives, goodness knows what she's doing with the loot because she sure as hell isn't selling it and living a life of luxury off the proceeds."

"And why would she steal pets when she won't even take her own back?"

"True."

"Hey," a voice came from behind me.

I squealed and jumped. For God's sake. "Don't do that!"

"Do what?" James asked innocently.

"Sneak up and give me a heart attack."

"I didn't exactly sneak—I walked normally. You might want to have a word with those dogs that won't shut up. If it wasn't for them, you would've heard me."

"Fair enough," I grumbled.

"Okay, kids, stop fighting, or I'll have to send you to your rooms." Will raised a brow.

"Please do. It'd be much better than standing here in the dark and cold and noise." My eyes widened. "What if she is home but had a fall or something? I'm worried about her welfare. Aren't you?" Okay, so I wasn't, and we all knew it.

Will gave me an assessing gaze. "We probably have to wait here a bit longer before we declare she might have hurt herself."

A man's voice from behind the neighbouring fence screamed, "Shut up! Shut those damned dogs up! I'm calling the police!"

"Should we just wait for the police to let us in?" I asked. "Can we at least wait in the Range Rover?"

"That might be the best idea you've had all night. Bags the front seat." James's white teeth flashed past me as he sprinted to the car, grinning the whole way. I took off quickly, but he beat me. Poo bum. We were both already in the car by the time Will slid into the front seat.

"You guys are ridiculous when you're together. This is the last time I do any assignments with you at the same time." Will shut his door, which went some way to drowning out the calamity of animal noise.

I rubbed my hands together to warm them. "Who wants

to take bets on whether Mrs Allingham or the police will get here first?"

A set of headlights shone into the driveway.

Folks, we had a winner.

An automatic garage door opened to the right of the house, a light coming on inside it. The car waiting to drive in was a dark coloured van. "Um, suspicious, or is it just me?"

"If she has lots of dogs, maybe she needs a van to run them to the vets and dog groomers?" James offered.

"I'm going with Lily on this one. I'd love to know what's in that van." A figure walked out from the garage, but as it was backlit, it was hard to make out who it was. I was putting my money on it being Mrs Allingham.

I squinted. "What the hell?" Was I seeing what I thought I was seeing?

Will and James both stared towards the garage. The door had started its slow descent, but the dodgy light from inside didn't just silhouette a person—there were various smaller and medium-sized forms on the ground around her. And what were the growths on her shoulder and back? I was sure she hadn't been hunchbacked last time we'd seen her.

James flicked his gaze towards me, and we shared a puzzled look. Will put his hand on his door. "Lily, wait here while James and I check it out."

"Do I have to?" I wanted to hear Mrs Allingham try and explain herself, and I wanted to know what she had with her. Were Gremlins real?

Will's voice was firm, and James gave me a look to back him up. "Yes, Lily, you have to. Come on, James."

By the time the boys got out, Mrs Allingham and her troupe of Gremlins had arrived at her front door. Will and James had almost reached her when a dog barked. In the middle of opening her door, she turned to see what the dog had been barking about. But it was dark. "Is someone there?" she called out over the barking dog.

Will said something that I couldn't make out—he was facing the wrong way, and my window was closed. Will's magic tickled my scalp. His hand glowed, the light strong enough to illuminate him, James, Mrs Allingham, and her… animals. Milling around her legs was a seething mass of dogs, cats, a ferret, and a…. Oh my God, yes, it *was* a monkey. Where the hell had she gotten a monkey from? And why? Was that even legal?

My hand rested on my door, itching to open it. Blooming instructions—gah, I hated following them. Thankfully, Will had left the key in the ignition, and I was able to lower my window so I could at least listen to what was going on.

Will had reached her, so he didn't have to talk as loudly, and the dogs were still barking. Damn. I couldn't hear anything interesting. Even though she could probably feel my magic, I drew on a small amount. "Send their voices to me so I can hear the conversation." I didn't just say "let me hear them" because I could've ended up transporting myself over there, and other than shocking the hell out of myself, I would've been in huge trouble with Will and James.

"That's ridiculous! What've you been smoking, young man?" Gee, the drug-taking accusations were rife this week.

Will answered, "Nothing, Mrs Allingham. Look, you're not in trouble—we just need to know why you lied to us."

"I'll call your superiors and make a complaint if you don't leave now. This is harassment. I told you before; I'm not Mrs Allingham. Now leave." A low growl rumbled across the driveway. Crap. One of her dogs was likely reacting to her stress. Will and James had better be careful.

Something glinted in the glow from Will's hand. I stuck my head out the window, trying to get a better look. Whatever it was, it was a shiny beacon, like a lighthouse, but much, much smaller, and nowhere near the water. Okay, so it wasn't like a lighthouse at all, but it was drawing my attention. One of the cats at her feet held the shiny implement in its mouth. Oh, wow, that lump on her shoulder was a cockatoo, and what did it have in its beak? It looked like a small penguin, like a kid's soft toy.

"We need to ask you some questions, Mrs Allingham." Will was still trying, bless his persistent little heart.

James interrupted. "Is your dog wearing a gold necklace?" He looked down at a medium-sized short-haired dog. I couldn't make out much more than that from here, but I sensed a theme emerging.

Was she our burglar? That would make total sense, as much as using animals to do your dirty work for you made sense. My mouth dropped open. That would be why I couldn't get photos of the person who was stealing everything, because they weren't people—they were animals!

Her laugh was a nervous machine-gun sound. "That's not gold. It's fake. She likes expensive-looking things."

James folded his arms. "She's a dog. Dogs don't think in terms of expense."

She raised her chin. "How do you know?"

Will stepped in. "Look, Mrs Allingham, you still need to answer the question: Why did you lie to us?"

Her angry tone rose above the dog barks. "Why are you asking so many questions?" A strange magic prickled my scalp—stubborn and almost painful, like half-strength bee stings. More dogs were slinking out of the house. What was she doing? She shot her hands straight up into the air and shouted, "Attack!"

A couple of the dogs howled but didn't move. Unfortunately, six others obeyed, as well as the monkey and a few cats. They leapt at Will and James, both men hurriedly constructing shields—I guessed they didn't want to hurt the animals. They were vicious but were likely being compelled. What was happening was not their fault. I cringed at every snarl, yowl, and snap. The cockatoo screeched and flapped, launching from the witch's shoulder to fly into the air and dive-bomb Will.

That creepy magic grew stronger as Will and James fought off the animals. It was hard work keeping their shields up. Every attack required more magic to fill the hole in the shield. And they couldn't run away—they still had to arrest Mrs Allingham, now that they had an outright reason to.

But she wasn't done yet. She was making a doorway.

Crap.

If she got away, we might never find her. I jumped out of the car—the future lecture I'd cop be damned—and sprinted towards them. Just as Mrs Allingham tied her magic off and prepared to walk through, I threw up my own doorway in front of her—I'd never made a doorway from such a distance and whilst running. *Please work.*

Without realising my doorway had popped up in front of hers, she walked through. I smiled and made a second doorway to where I'd hopefully sent her.

The PIB reception room.

As I ran through, Will yelled, "Lily!" But there was no time. If I didn't get to her quickly, she could travel somewhere else.

Everything shifted as I came through to a familiar white room and bumped into Mrs Allingham. She stumbled forward but kept her feet. Thank goodness she was here and not somewhere else. Slapping those numbers on a doorway in a hurry had been tricky.

She steadied herself and spun towards me, her plaits flying with the force of it. "What the hell did you do? Where am I?"

How could I prolong this and give the guys enough time to get here with their magic-blocking handcuffs? Also, note to self—*don't* kill her. It was a sad day when you had to set yourself that reminder. I'd just have to do as they did in all the movies—keep her talking until help arrived or figure out a way to tie her up with magic. I looked at her with my second sight—she didn't have a return to sender up. Maybe she didn't know about them? I supposed not every witch did, especially if they weren't in law enforcement. "You're at PIB headquarters."

She narrowed her eyes. "How dare you take me some-where against my will! That's kidnapping."

"At least we know why you lied to us, Mrs Allingham. A cat burglar who uses actual cats to do the job. Clever." A bit of praise never hurt anyone. Maybe she'd relax a bit so I could take her unawares.

Her magic tingled my scalp—what was she up to? I was ready if she made a doorway, and I had my return to sender up, so I was relatively safe. "I told you before: I'm not Mrs Allingham. Would you get that through your daft head?"

"Sorry, no can do. I can understand why you stole the jewellery, but why the pets?"

She looked at me, a scowl firmly embedded, then threw her hands towards me, gushes of scalding flame hitting my shield.

Crap.

The flame bounced off my magic and slammed into her. Her grey plaits caught fire, and her clothes flamed. I drew on my magic and shouted, "Drench Mrs Allingham." If she really wasn't Mrs Allingham, she was going to be burnt toast in about thirty seconds, and Will, James, and I were going to be in a world of trouble. I held my breath.

Water appeared above her and dumped on her head, dousing the flames. I blew my breath out. A white washcloth covered her face, and a rubber ducky fell onto the floor with the torrent. Water splashed my legs. Oops. Some unsuspecting person was sitting in an empty bath about now, wondering where the hell their water and bath accoutrements had just gone. I so hoped it was a witch; otherwise, they'd probably need therapy for life. So even though I'd saved Mrs Allingham, I was still going to get in trouble. Some days, you just couldn't win.

"How did you do that?" Her eyes were wide, her voice part incredulous, part livid.

"Do what?"

"Don't be cute. Turn my magic on me!"

I shrugged, hoping my attempt at being casual was coming off. "Ah, that. I wasn't sure if you meant the water thing." Her jaw clenched. Me dragging this out was sending her into volcano mode. Now, to top it off. "It's a secret."

"Tell me!" She lunged towards me, arms outstretched. Her hands gripped my throat and squeezed, long nails digging in.

She pushed me back, and I grabbed her hands, trying to dislodge them. "Stop…. I can't"—*cough*—"breathe"—*cough*. She squeezed harder. Pain radiated around my neck and lanced into my throat. This really sucked.

*Concentrate. Ignore the need to breathe.* I needed to come up with a spell that wouldn't kill her. I shut it all out and drew on my power. *Make her punch herself in the face.*

Mrs Allingham released my throat, and I sucked in air in between coughing bouts. She, on the other hand—or was that on both hands, ha ha—punched herself first in the right eye, then in the left eye. She screamed and fell back, punching herself in the face again. I straightened. If I didn't stop this soon, she'd knock herself out. I rubbed my aching neck. "Stop Mrs Allingham from punching herself."

The door opened, and Gus poked his head in. "Miss Lily?" He noticed Mrs Allingham. "Who's that?"

"Shut the door, Gus. She's dangerous." As if she agreed with me, Mrs Allingham growled.

Gus raised his brows. "I have a gun."

"No. We'll never hear the end of it if I manage to get her killed. My magic will be enough."

"You sure?"

"Positive."

"Okay, then. Don't say I didn't ask." He shut the door.

She stilled, looking at me with murder in her blackened eyes, the skin around them already swelling. Her magic prickled my scalp again. Instead of casting a spell, she made a doorway.

Not again. Why couldn't witches just admit when they were beaten?

"Stop!" I called out. She froze midstep. I concentrated on her doorway. "Dissolve." I blinked. It actually had. Go, me. Her attempts at unfreezing herself drained my magic. I wasn't sure how much longer I could hold her here before I collapsed. Had I just made a huge mistake?

"Lily!" Will stepped through his doorway, took stock of the situation, and ran to Mrs Allingham.

I unfroze Mrs Allingham so Will could wrench her arms behind her back and handcuff her.

"Where's James?" I rasped out.

"He's gathering evidence and all the animals. We put a

call into here, and three agents are on the way to help him."
He looked down at Mrs Allingham. "You're under arrest on
suspicion of burglary, animal-napping, and mind-control of
animals to commit theft. You do not have to say anything,
but it may harm your defence if you do not mention when
questioned something which you later rely on in court.
Anything you do say may be given in evidence."

She tried to struggle out of his grip, but she couldn't.
Will gave her another once over—she looked like a drowned
rat that had gone ten rounds with a cat—then stared at me,
one eyebrow raised. "What happened?"

"Um, she attacked me with fire, which bounced off my
protection spell." I wasn't going to say more than that. No
need to give our secrets away. "So to stop her burning to
death, I called water from... somewhere." My traitorous
gaze strayed to the rubber ducky.

Will followed my gaze. His eyes widened. He looked up
at me, about to say something, but I cut him off. "Don't, or
I'll turn your Range Rover back."

"You wouldn't!"

I smiled. "I totally would. Anyway, I haven't finished the
story yet. See these marks." I lifted my chin, took my tie off
so I could loosen my shirt, and showed him my neck. His
brow furrowed. "When magic wouldn't work, she tried to
strangle me, so I had to get out of it without killing her, and
so I made her punch herself. I haven't laid a hand on her.
She did all of this to herself."

Fury swelled in Mrs Allingham's eyes until I thought
they would pop out of her head. "She's lying."

Will nodded at the security camera. "I guess we'll soon find out. Oh, and you're also under arrest for assaulting a PIB contractor. Come on." He buzzed the intercom, and Gus opened the door.

As we waited for the lift, Will called Beren and organised for him to meet me at the infirmary. When Will and Gus took Mrs Allingham down, I took the next lift up. After Beren checked me out and magicked away the bruising, I was good to go, but I wanted to find out the full extent of the animal situation. How many animals had she stolen?

I grabbed some dinner from the cafeteria while I waited. After an hour, my phone rang. "Hey, sis. I heard what happened. Are you okay?"

"Yeah, I'm fine, just bored now waiting for you two. I want to know the full story."

"Glad to hear you're okay. I'm driving Will's car back. I'll be there in fifteen minutes. See you in my office, then. Bye."

"Bye."

I hurried upstairs to his office and called Will. He was still dealing with Mrs Allingham and told me to get James to wait. So much waiting. It was as if the universe wanted to annoy me for fun. I didn't appreciate it. It had been a long day, and after using all that magic, then eating a scrumptious beef vindaloo and rice, a nap was looking like a good idea. I found a spot behind James's desk, magicked a cushion from Angelica's house to myself, and lay on the floor. I would've magicked my whole bed, but I didn't have the energy, and there was nowhere to fit it…. Hmm, I could get rid of James's table. Yeah, nah, there was no way I had the power to do all that and not kill myself.

I must have drifted off because something wet and gross in my ear woke me. "Argh, stop." I slapped at the side of my face and opened my eyes. Will was kneeling next to me, laughing. He stuck his finger in the air. "Ew, yuck. You gave me a wet willie, didn't you?"

"You know it."

"So childish."

"I had to put up with you two being ridiculous in my car; the least I could do was level the playing field." He turned and high-fived my brother.

"Come on, Lily. Get up. I want to get to my chair, and you're blocking the way." My brother had no empathy sometimes.

"Yeah, yeah." I sat up and wiped the dribble from the side of my chin. I was so gross. How Will was still around was a wonder. I should be nicer to him. I stood and moved to one of the guest chairs on the other side of James's table, hugging the cushion to me when I sat. Will sat next to me, grinning and waving his finger. I narrowed my eyes. "Keep that thing away from me."

He moved it close to my ear, and I swatted it away—it was like being attacked by a mosquito. I was sure I could hear buzzing. The second time he waved it at me, I magicked my beanie to myself and onto my head. It covered my ears. Will sighed. "You're no fun."

"Okay, you two. Time to get to work. Don't you want to know what I discovered?"

"Of course." I sat up straighter and shook my head. I wasn't quite awake. Five minutes of sleep was a terrible thing to do to yourself.

"There were thirty-seven animals living in that house of horrors."

My mouth dropped open. "Oh my God. That's beyond comprehension."

"Tell me about it. I can still smell the stench on my clothes." James pulled a disgusted face. "We found all the missing animals from the burglaries, except Mrs Horsham's cat, of course." I sighed out a mixture of relief and sadness. Yay that so many animals had been found, but poor Mervin.

"Fiona will be happy," said Will.

I rolled my eyes and affected a sugary-sweet voice. "Don't you mean *Fee*?" He shook his head but made no comment.

"We got our hands on a microchip reader and found many of the animals were from the same shelter you and Mill got Cinnamon and Bagel from."

"Oh my God. They'd just been cleaned out the week or two before we went. Wow."

"Yeah. Those animals will all end up back there, I'm afraid, except for a black Labrador that Agent Peters fell in love with." He smiled, but then he frowned, two little lines appearing between his eyes. "There were a few deceased pets too. Looks like she killed the ones that didn't cooperate, which is probably what happened to Mervin. We've deciphered the spells and called Millicent to the scene. She spoke to a few of the animals and found that they were compelled, and any who resisted were zapped dead. That white cat escaped—it was apparently a gift from a friend a few years ago. We were lucky she never thought to get rid of Marshmallow's microchip. Anyway, when the alarm went off in Mr Painter's house, the other animals ran out, and Mrs Allingham couldn't hang around outside and wait, but Marshmallow hid." Marshmallow was a smart cat.

I leaned forward. "So she was using them to steal stuff, and that's why weird, worthless things were taken?"

"Yes. She let the animals take something they liked as long as they got what she wanted as well. They're like little kids."

My heart dropped, and tears burnt my eyes. Those poor animals. They were looking for love and a home, and all they got was compelled and abused. Why were people so evil? I swallowed my sadness and blinked back the tears. "Maybe I should adopt one?"

Will whiplashed his head around to look at me. "What? And what's this *I* business? I thought we were a team?"

"Well, we are a team, but this is something I really want, and I was going to do it whether you wanted me to or not. Sorry."

"Don't say that, Lily. You're not in the least bit sorry." He laughed. "It's okay, though, because your heart is in the right place, and I happen to agree with your crazy idea."

"Yay!" I grinned and leaned over to give Will a big kiss on the cheek. I may also have licked him too because I knew he'd hate it, and I owed him one for the wet willie.

He screwed up his face. "Gross."

I smirked. "I know." I looked at James. "When will the animals be back in the shelter?"

"Tomorrow afternoon. Why don't you both go, and take Millicent with you—she can aid the interview process." He laughed.

Excitement had replaced some of the sadness. "Great idea."

"Anyway, we've got agents cataloguing the loot—they're still at the house—and all the animals are staying at three different vets. We're paying for them to all get a looking over and any treatment they might need with one of the local witch vets. We're also working to disable the spells. They should all be ready to rehome and go back to their owners by tomorrow night."

"Do we know why she did it?" I asked. I mean, we could assume it was because she was a hoarder and just plain evil, but it would be nice to know for sure.

James ran a hand through his hair. "Millicent was able to get an idea from talking to the monkey. He'd been with her for two years. She stole him from the London Zoo." Wow, magic in the wrong hands was terrible. "She hated anyone who was doing better than her, especially if they happened to be non-witches."

"Oh, so 95 percent of other people?" Will said.

"Yeah, something like that. Stealing people's prized possessions gave her power. She enjoyed the fact that she was causing them pain, but also she had power over them in some way. And the animals did her bidding, also making her feel important. She was angry when they took her son away, more because they took control away from her, not because she loved him. To be honest, listening to Millicent translate some of the information was chilling. There are things I won't mention because they're under investigation now, but in regards to thefts, we think her using animals to steal things started about a year ago. Before that, she did it by herself."

Will shook his head. "Sounds like a true psychopath. At least she's now in jail, where she belongs." Will looked at me. "Thanks mainly to you, and you managed not to kill our suspect this time. Nice work."

"Gee, thanks." I smiled anyway because he was right. "You guys were defending yourselves, and she made a doorway. I couldn't do too much else because I was too far away from her." I gave them both a narrow-eyed glance before continuing. "But, thankfully, I was able to stick my doorway in front of hers as she stepped through, and she ended up here."

James watched me with an assessing gaze. "I know I say this every time, but you really surprise me sometimes, and if Ma'am were here, she'd be proud too. Great work."

"Thanks. Where is she, by the way?" I hadn't seen her at all today, and it seemed as if I'd seen less and less of her over the last two weeks.

"They're keeping her busy, but don't worry. She's fine." I'd have to take my brother's word for it. "Anyway, time for all of us to go home and get some rest. You two have a big afternoon ahead of you tomorrow, choosing a fur baby." He smiled.

"I can't wait! We'll have to pick an animal that will get along with the rats because Bagel might come and visit sometimes."

Will snorted. "Before you know it, we'll have a zoo. You watch." He stood. "Come on, Lily, let's go home."

I stood. "Night, Jay." I gave my brother a quick hug. "Can you ask Mill to meet me at the shelter at four? Will the animals be there then?"

"Yeah, they should be. If there's any change, I'll let you know. Night."

We made our doorways, and as we stepped through, excitement at having something to actually look forward to tomorrow zinged through me. Wonders would never cease.

# CHAPTER 14

So here we were again, at the Feathered and Furry Friends Animal Shelter. Will and I held hands as we wandered in between rows of now-full cages. So many gorgeous faces who needed love. Thankfully, there was a family with two young kids, and a middle-aged woman also looking for a fur baby. I crossed my fingers that these animals would all have homes soon.

"Would you prefer a dog or a cat?" Millicent asked.

I'd tossed and turned all night, wondering what to get, but I had no idea. "I don't know. Dogs need a lot of work, like walking and picking up poo, but even though cats are affectionate and easy to manage, you can't take them with you when you go out. I'm not sure. I was kind of hoping one of the animals would jump out at me as being *the one*."

"What about you, Will?"

"I don't know. Whatever Lily wants is fine with me." Aw, I was so lucky.

When we'd done a whole lap of the cages, it struck me. "Marshmallow Kitty Allingham isn't here."

Millicent smiled. "James mentioned her. Apparently, the agent who had her overnight decided to keep her."

"That's awesome!" Joy crowded my heart at that news. That gorgeous cat would have someone to love her. Hopefully it would make up for being trapped by Mrs Allingham.

"Meow." A cat called from a few cages away. I walked over. The long-haired brown-and-white cat rubbed its side along the cage. The brown fur covered its head and eyes, but stopped just under its eyes, like a Zorro mask. Quite cool.

"Are you asking for a pat?" I bent and gave her a scratch through the bars. Also in the cage was a tan-coloured medium-sized scruff ball. I straightened and looked at Jane, the woman who ran the place. "Do you usually put cats and dogs in the same cages?"

"No. We tried to separate them, but the cat—a she— wouldn't leave his side. They're both desexed by the way."

"Interesting." Will also bent and gave the cat a scratch. She purred, and the dog stood and inched towards us.

I squatted. "Hey, boy, come here. It's okay." He stopped and watched me with huge timid eyes. "Poor thing. He's scared." I expected Millicent to step in, but she stayed back. Maybe she didn't want to interfere? I wasn't really sure how this stuff worked. "Come on, gorgeous boy." I made kissy noises. The cat looked at him as if to say, come on, silly. He sniffed the air, then came up to the bars, sticking his wet nose up to sniff my hand. "That's right; check me out. If you come home with us, we'll give you all the love and treats, but you'll have to have a bath." He cocked his head to the side as if he were listening. "I'm Lily, and this is Will. We're awesome. Really we are." Millicent giggled. "She thinks we're awesome too. She's just trying to be funny. Do you guys like rats?" The cat swished her tail from side to side. "If you come home with us, you have to be nice to rats too. We have a couple who are friends, and if they visit, I want them to be safe."

Jane was probably rethinking allowing us to take any animals home by this stage. Maybe I should stop talking.

Will gave the cat another scratch. "So, you two, what's the verdict? Do you want to come home with me and the crazy lady?"

The dog whined, wagged his tail, and licked me. The cat purred louder. Seemed like they'd made their choice. I turned and looked up at Millicent, just to make sure. She gave a smile and a nod, and my heart soared.

I stood and smiled at Jane. "We'll have these two thanks."

Jane's smile was huge. "That's wonderful news! I'm so happy they're being adopted together. Congratulations."

Will stood and put his arm around me. "So, Lily, we have two fur kids. Happy now?"

I beamed, and my stomach warmed with emotion. These two would be the most loved animals on the planet.

"Couldn't be happier." Was this the next step in our relationship? Were we really getting fur babies together?

He planted a kiss on my forehead. "Neither could I." Hmm, I guessed we were.

Millicent grinned. "They both said they couldn't be happier either." Jane laughed, thinking it was a joke, but Will and I knew better. If they'd come from Mrs Allingham, they'd been exposed to her brain. I shuddered. It meant they knew how horrible some people were, but it also meant they could understand what we said. That was doubly cool. Now I just had to take Millicent up on her offer to teach me how to understand them.

And just like that, our family of two became four. I was normally terrible at maths, but this was the kind of arithmetic I could get on board with. I bent down and looked in the cage again. Both animals stared at me, and I could've sworn they were smiling.

Warmth blossomed in my chest. "Okay, you two. Let's go home."

And we did.

# ALSO BY DIONNE LISTER

## *Paranormal Investigation Bureau*

*Witchnapped in Westerham #1*

*Witch Swindled in Westerham #2*

*Witch Undercover in Westerham #3*

*Witchslapped in Westerham #4*

*Witch Silenced in Westerham #5*

*Killer Witch in Westerham #6*

*Witch Haunted in Westerham #7*

*Witch Oracle in Westerham #8*

*Witchbotched in Westerham #9*

*Witch Cursed in Westerham #10*

*Witch Heist in Westerham #11*

*Vampire Witch in Westerham #13*

*Witch War in Westerham #14*

## *The Circle of Talia*

(YA Epic Fantasy)

*Shadows of the Realm*

*A Time of Darkness*

*Realm of Blood and Fire*

### The Rose of Nerine

(Epic Fantasy)

*Tempering the Rose*

# ABOUT THE AUTHOR

I'm sure you know me by now if you've gotten this far in the series. I love writing stuff, but I won't bore you with the rest of it. If you want to find me, I'm on Facebook, Twitter, and Instagram, oh, and I also have a website https://dionnelisterwriter.com.

Printed in Great Britain
by Amazon

73495338R00125